and
The Blackrobes

BOOK·ONE

DEATH & DUPLICITY

PATRICK TRESE

Verisimilitude, in my book, trumps factuality.

This novel mixes fiction and fact. It tells the stories of make-believe men and women who became involved with real people in actual major events. Those real people who spoke to my fictional characters said what I wanted them to say. So did the characters I created until they began to say and do whatever they wished. It happens and, as one of my imagined persons reminded me, it's strange how some things work out. Amen?

DEATH & DUPLICITY

July 17, 2019

For Kate —

—◦•➢•➢•✦•ᴄ•ᴄ•◦—

With much love and
gratitude for a wonderful
friendship,

Patrick

CHAPTER · 1

THE WINDS OF CHANGE were blowing through the streets of Moscow. Russians were moving cautiously, eyes averted. Much was being left unsaid.

It was February 27, 1956.

Two days before, so it was whispered, Nikita Khrushchev had stood before the Communist Party Congress and vigorously denounced Stalin and his reign of terror. The speech had been delivered in secret, but enough fragments had leaked out to panic Captain Oksana Volkova of the Chief Intelligence Directorate of the General Staff of the Red Army.

Fighting the gusts of cold air that sliced through her heavy overcoat, she rushed through corridors of snow piled high along the sidewalks. Her general had summoned her and she dared not be late. She skidded around an icy corner, but kept her balance and did not fall.

Up ahead loomed the headquarters of her special division of the GRU. Beyond its iron gates stood the ancient gray mansion surrounded by its black, leafless trees. Her wristwatch was buried beneath her winter gloves, but she reckoned it was at least ten minutes before ten o'clock. She paused, squared her shoulders and marched through the open gates toward the sentries standing guard in the colonnade.

General Michail Andreyevich Kalenko stood waiting for her in the entrance hall, his overcoat draped over his arm. She whipped the glove off her right hand and saluted.

"Am I late, General?"

"No, Captain. You are punctual. As always."

General Kalenko threw his overcoat around his shoulders like a cloak.

"Turn around," he said. "We shall take a walk."

He ushered her out the front door, across the porch and down the steps. He did not speak until they were beyond earshot of the sentries.

"It's intolerable in there," he said. "For two days nobody has said anything. Not inside the building, at any rate. You have heard about Khrushchev's speech?"

"Just rumors, General."

"Well, I was there when he made it. Damned frightening, let me tell you!" He spat into the snow. "Khrushchev! Where was this ignorant upstart's voice when Stalin was alive? This Khrushchev had the audacity to stand there and pontificate with such malice. What is frightening is that nobody has dared to challenge him!"

"What about Bulganin and Molotov and Malenkov and the rest?"

"Yes, what about them? Silent, so far. They wanted to

block his ascendency, but they waited too long. Only last year he was sharing power with Bulganin. 'Co-equals' the Western press called them. The celebrated B-and-K. But no more. Khrushchev has managed to make sure there is no B. Only the K."

They reached a slippery patch of sidewalk and stopped short of the edge.

"We have to discuss your project," said the General. "How does it progress?"

"It goes slowly, but steadily. I make good progress every day."

"I fear that good is no longer good enough, Oksana. Stalin appreciated the patient, subtle game. But Khrushchev is impulsive. If he continues ruling unchecked, time is not our friend. Your clock must run faster."

He strode forward across the sheet of ice. "Khrushchev is ignorant and therefore impatient. He is abusive and shrewd and dangerous. Arrogant, ignorant, reckless. Much too provocative and relentless, this Khrushchev. He will destroy us."

"Destroy the GRU, General?"

"The world, Captain! I fear he will destroy the world. There will come a day when this arrogant fool Khrushchev will push the United States too hard and too far. Once Eisenhower leaves office, who in America will be able to deal with this Khrushchev? Eisenhower understands war. Therefore, he knows how to avoid it. But what does this Nixon know?"

"You believe the vice-president will succeed Eisenhower?"

"If not Nixon, some fool like him. Eisenhower is the last man of substance the Americans have. Whoever takes his place will most certainly be a shallow politician, no better than Khrushchev with little understanding of the power at his disposal. The bluffs and threats of two such blockheads will cause them to lose what little self-control they possess. Pride and ignorance cause irrational decisions to be made and can destroy both our nations. I do not exaggerate! Both nations have more than enough weapons to destroy our planet. That real possibility is beyond Khrushchev's comprehension."

The General stopped walking.

"How far can you take your project, do you think? To what level?"

"It depends on circumstances, General. It may all fall apart and fail. But the possibilities are without limit."

"You have determined what must be done in the United States? Every last detail?"

"I believe so, General."

"Then let us continue to assume that it will work, Oksana. It could turn out to be critical. Win or lose, it is time to get started. Go there and prepare the ground as soon as possible. We are facing a perilous future, Oksana, and our time is running out."

*   *   *

SEVERAL WEEKS LATER, CAPTAIN Volkova, traveling under an assumed name, joined the staff of the Soviet Embassy in Ottawa. Documents submitted to the Canadian government certified that she was a stenographer and research assistant. She stayed inside the embassy until one Thursday morning when she joined several other Russian women from the embassy staff on a shopping tour of the city. Shortly before noon, she rendezvoused with a resident agent, an American woman her own age. In the ladies room of Ottawa's largest department store, Captain Volkova changed her shoes, slipped into the other woman's raincoat, adjusted the wig she had carried in her purse, put on a pair of glasses, and checked her new image in the mirror. Satisfied, she left the store with her new companion.

They walked two blocks to a public garage where the American woman had parked her automobile, a light blue sedan with New York license plates. Once inside the car, the woman gave her a well-used wallet.

"Tuck that away in your purse," she said. "It has all the documents you'll need: driver's license, birth certificate, Social Security card, library card, that sort of thing. No need for a passport, as you know. You are Lydia Chalmers, my old college roommate from Dayton, Ohio. I'm Joan Cunningham from Buffalo, New York. Your clothes and toilet articles are packed in a suitcase in the trunk. There's also a shopping bag with a sweater and some knick-knacks you bought here in Canada. Nothing expensive. The travel brochures in the glove compartment will give you an idea of where we've been on our vacation, in case anybody asks."

"Do you have a weapon?"

"I won't be given one until we cross the border and clear customs. Don't worry; I've done this before. I'll have a gun when we need it."

They left Ottawa and drove west to Toronto, then followed Lake Huron southeast to Niagara Falls. The two women, "American tourists returning from vacation with nothing much to declare" crossed the Rainbow Bridge and entered the United States without incident. From Buffalo, they traveled south through New York State into northern Pennsylvania.

Throughout this part of the trip, Oksana Volkova studied the way the traffic moved along the streets of the towns and cities they passed through, examined the goods for sale in the stores, took snapshots of street signs, mailboxes, traffic lights, fire hydrants and telephone booths. She kept a notebook in which she wrote down overheard slang words and idiomatic expressions. By the time they approached the town of Bellefonte in Pennsylvania, she had filled two shopping bags with copies of the local newspapers, illustrated travel guides, church bulletins, handbills, ticket stubs and restaurant menus. They cruised down Bellefonte's tree-lined Main Street that sunny morning, turned right onto a shady avenue, and then turned left into a smaller side street.

"That's the house," said Oksana, who had been checking the numbers on the modest homes. "There! That red brick house on the right."

The resident agent glanced at the house and nodded. She did not slow down.

Later that afternoon, the two women joined a group of tourists and took a boat ride through Penn's Cave near the village of Centre Hall. A middle-aged couple took the seat behind them.

"Reminds me of the old poem," said the man as the flat-bottomed boat floated through the subterranean stalagmite forest.

He leaned forward and recited softly: "'Where Alph, the sacred river, ran through caverns measureless to man, down to a sunless sea.' Wordsworth," the man said.

The resident agent turned her head slightly. "I believe it was Coleridge."

"Really? All these years I thought it was Wordsworth."

"No, Coleridge," the resident agent said firmly. "Samuel Taylor Coleridge."

"Well, thank you," said the man. "I'll try to remember that."

"Please do," said the resident agent. "Here, I think you dropped this." She handed him the key to the trunk of her blue sedan.

"Ah, yes, thank you," said the man. "I'm very much obliged."

After the tour of the caverns ended, the two women spent several minutes in the souvenir shop before returning to their car. The resident agent retrieved the key from under the floor mat. "You can check the trunk, if you want to," said the resident agent, "but I'm sure what we need is there."

"Very well," said Oksana. "Let's be on our way."

They ate a leisurely dinner at a rustic tavern perched on the summit of Nittany Mountain. From their booth by a window, they watched the dusk creep across the checkerboard fields below. They quietly discussed the house in Bellefonte. The hedge running alongside the driveway was high enough to cut off the neighbors' view of the side door. They'd be able to get in and out without being seen.

They lingered over coffee and walnut pie until it was dark and then drove down the mountain. At the first service station, they made certain that their gas tank was full. The resident agent asked the attendant to check the oil and water and the air pressure in the tires. When he finished, she paid him in cash.

Driving along a back road, they found a clearing in the woods where hunters, so said the resident agent, parked their vehicles during deer season. They changed clothes in the dark. They put their skirts and shoes in the trunk of the car, put on gray coveralls, tucked their hair under workmen's caps and laced up sturdy boots.

"Let's not forget the present our friends left us," said the resident agent.

She took a shoebox from the trunk and put it on the front seat of the car. Oksana lifted the lid of the box. The firearm was inside. Before getting back on the road, they replaced the car's New York license plates with license plates from Pennsylvania.

CHAPTER · 2

AT TEN O'CLOCK THAT night, while the resident agent waited in the car, Oksana made a call from a public telephone booth on Bellefonte's Main Street.

"Mrs. Vogel?" she said when the woman answered. "My name is Helen Haywood. You do not know me, but I must see you tonight. Yes, I know it's late, but I have news of your brother. Yes, the very one. But for God's sake, don't tell anyone, whatever you do. I am very frightened to do this. I can't be seen. The side door? Good. Yes, good, Mrs. Vogel. I am so glad I can trust you to keep my visit secret. My sister is driving me. She says we can be there in five minutes."

She climbed back into the car. "She's waiting for us. Pull right up into the driveway. She'll meet us at the side door."

The resident agent handed her a pair of the thin rubber gloves surgeons wear in operating rooms. Oksana Volkova slipped them on and flexed her fingers. "Good fit," she said.

MRS. VOGEL WAS A stout woman of medium height, grey hair, in her late sixties. She stood at the top of the steps to the side door of her house, peering through plain, gold-rimmed spectacles. She was clutching her pink quilted bathrobe at the neck.

Oksana entered first. "Forgive our disguises, Mrs. Vogel," she said. "We cannot take the chance of being discovered. Our lives depend on it. And we must hurry. This is my sister, Martha."

The woman tried to greet her visitors, but Oksana urged her back into the kitchen.

"Hurry. We must not be seen," she told the woman.

The resident agent, carrying the shoebox, edged around them and hurried toward the living room.

"The blinds are all drawn downstairs," she reported. "I'll go upstairs and check the bedrooms."

"Don't forget the bathroom!" Oksana called back.

"What is going on?" said the woman. "You can't just come barging in here!"

"Forgive me," said Oksana Volkova, forcing the woman backward into her own home. "We must make certain that we are not observed. You must understand. The nature of this business makes it necessary."

"But I don't understand . . ."

"Please! There is not much time. It is about your brother."

Oksana kept moving Mrs. Vogel backward into the living room.

"The second floor is clear," the resident agent called down from the top of the stairs. "Use the bedroom on your right. It's much larger."

"Who are you?" cried Mrs. Vogel. She seemed unable to move.

"All in good time. I have news. Upstairs," said Oksana firmly, turning the woman toward the stairway. "We will talk upstairs. About your brother. Quickly now."

She pushed the woman up the staircase and into the bedroom. The resident agent was waiting there, holding a pillowcase.

"Here," she said. "Put this over your head."

The woman stared at her wide eyed.

"Put it on. Don't you want to hear about your brother? Then slip this over your head. Quickly, now."

The woman did as she was told. "I don't see why this is necessary," she whined.

Oksana Volkova sat next to her on the bed with her arm around the woman's shoulder.

The resident agent cut a length of window cord to hold the pillowcase in place and tied it around the woman's neck. "Hold her tightly, now," she said.

Mrs. Vogel struggled, but she did not scream.

"What are you doing?" she said. "What are you doing to me?"

The resident agent screwed a silencing device onto the barrel of her gun.

Mrs. Vogel began whimpering. "My glasses have fallen off. Please, my glasses!"

Oksana Volkova put her mouth close to the woman's head.

"Listen carefully. Your brother is alive. For now, he is safe. Just relax and listen."

"Why do you have my head covered? Why are you treating me so roughly?"

"Only to make things safer, Mrs. Vogel. Please just sit quietly. I will explain everything to you."

Oksana stood up and moved a few steps from the bed. The resident agent fired. The pillow case flushed red. Mrs. Vogel collapsed onto the bed. A dark red pool spread out around her head and seeped into the bedspread.

"Well done," said Oksana.

She checked the dead woman's pulse. "No blood on either one of us."

The resident agent, breathing slowly and deeply, stood staring at the body on the bed.

"I'm always surprised how quickly life ends," she said. "Instantly."

Without taking her eyes off the corpse, the resident agent unscrewed the silencer from the barrel of the gun and put the weapon back into the shoebox. She looked at her wristwatch.

"Twenty after ten," she said. "What now?"

"Start collecting small items," said Oksana. "Anything a thief would carry away. Put them in the kitchen and we'll take them out to the car later. I will be looking for documents, photographs, letters and so forth. When you find such things, call me so I can examine them. Remember: the house should look ransacked, not searched."

Oksana went through each room, each closet, each drawer, each box, each pocket. She examined each note, each letter, each snapshot. She opened each book and shook out whatever was tucked between the pages. From time to time, she would place a note or a newspaper clipping or a snapshot on a smooth surface and photograph it with the small camera she wore on a strap around her neck. Then she would put the item back into the book or box or drawer exactly as she had found it.

She completed her exploration of the first floor on schedule and turned off the living room lights at eleven thirty-five. A neighbor or passerby would assume that Mrs. Vogel had finished watching the news on television and had gone upstairs to bed.

On the second floor, Oksana found the family album. She took the time to photograph every page. In the attic, she looked through six cardboard cartons and the drawers of an old bureau, but found nothing of interest. She took her flashlight and went down into the basement.

There was a workbench standing against one of the whitewashed walls. Above the workbench, the late Professor Vogel's tools were arranged neatly on pegboard. Her light flicked past a gas furnace, a hot water tank, an electric washer and dryer, a large double sink. Oksana looked carefully through a closet where Mrs. Vogel stored her canned goods. The basement, like the attic, was tidy and orderly as if it had recently been cleaned out. She found no books, photos or documents stored in the cellar.

"I checked the garage," said the resident agent when Oksana reached the top of the basement stairs. "Very clean. Nothing much in it except the woman's old Pontiac. Storm windows, garden hose, snow shovel. The usual stuff. Nothing in the trunk of her car except the jack and a spare tire. I left the trunk lid up and the car door open. I messed up the glove compartment and left the car keys on the front seat. What do you want to do with her purse?"

"Dump it out on the dining room table and take any money you find. We're finished here."

It was one o'clock in the morning. Working without light, the two women moved the burglary loot from the kitchen to the car. Oksana Volkova made one last tour of the house. They had left a convincing mess, but no clues.

"Where's the gun?" she asked when she returned to the kitchen.

"In our car. On the floor under the front seat. Don't worry," said the resident agent. "I never leave anything behind. Only the body."

THE TWO WOMEN DROVE out of Bellefonte and headed west toward Ohio and Michigan. Along the way, they stopped in the woods and changed their clothes. Driving on, they disposed of all the items they had taken from Mrs. Vogel's house, a little bit here, a little bit there. They ate an early breakfast at a rural drive-in restaurant and, before leaving the parking lot, tossed their boots and coveralls into the dumpster out back.

The gun used to kill Mrs. Vogel ended up submerged in an abandoned quarry along with its silencer. One by one, the coins from her husband's collection were redistributed to waitresses, cashiers, panhandlers and shopkeepers. Others were dropped into church poor boxes.

After stops in Cincinnati and Detroit, they headed north to Port Huron, Michigan, and drove across the Blue Water Bridge to Sarnia, Ontario. The officers on duty waved them across the border without question: just two more American tourists starting off on a Canadian vacation. They headed east toward Ottawa.

Two nights later, eleven women from the Soviet embassy went to a movie theater to see *The King and I* with Yul Brynner and Deborah Kerr. Oksana and the resident agent entered the theater a few minutes after the main feature started and went directly to the ladies room. There, Oksana removed her glasses and her wig and changed into Russian shoes. The resident agent stuffed her American raincoat, wig and shoes into a shopping bag. Oksana left without a word and walked down the aisle to where the Russian women were sitting. She slipped into the seat they had saved for her. A few minutes later, the resident agent took a seat in the back of the theater and sat through the rest of the film alone.

That night, having enjoyed the movie and a dish of ice cream at the restaurant down the street, Captain Oksana Volkova walked through the doors of the Soviet embassy with the other Russian women and disappeared. The resident agent spent the night in a hotel in Ottawa. Next morning, she drove back across the border to the United States to await her next assignment.

OKSANA VOLKOVA RETURNED TO the Soviet Union in September.

"Before leaving Canada," she told General Kalenko as they walked away from GRU headquarters, "I took the opportunity to watch an American political convention on television. The Democrats, not the Republicans."

"And you saw something that intrigued you," said the General. "Or should I say somebody?"

Oksana smiled.

"His name is John Kennedy. A wealthy young senator from Massachusetts. He almost won the nomination for vice-president. His supporters fought hard for him. You could see that on the television: people running up and down the aisles, people arguing, the cries and shouts as the leaders of the various states called out their votes. Very exciting."

"But he lost," said the General.

"He lost this time. By only 17 votes. Next time, I think it will be a different story. He will run for president himself in 1960, so people in America seem to believe. He won't have Eisenhower to contend with."

"True," said General Kalenko. "No one can beat Eisenhower this November. Adlai Stevenson lost to him last time and he will lose again this time."

General Kalenko said nothing for a few moments.

"So you believe this Kennedy might become President of the United States? In just four years, Oksana?"

"He's an impressive young man, General, and a Roman Catholic, as well. Intelligent, charming, somewhat ruthless they say. I think he will run and I think he will win."

"It's a gamble, I know," said the General. "But if this Kennedy becomes the American president? He might be worth waiting for. It is always better to do something—even the wrong thing—than do nothing and be destroyed. If your project falls apart, Oksana, nothing is lost. But you have identified a suitable target, so keep pushing forward and take the steps to reach it."

He clasped her by the shoulders.

"Good work, Major Volkova."

CHAPTER · 3

THE PATROL CAR WAS parked in front of the house on the tree-lined street of the small Pennsylvania town. It was a routine call. The two uniformed officers had walked up the driveway and stood outside the side door.

"It's unlocked," said the younger policeman. He pushed open the door and listened. "I don't hear anything, Jake."

"Then go ahead and let her know we're here."

"Mrs. Vogel? It's me! Cecil Moore! Are you okay? Your friends asked us to check and see if you're okay!"

There was no reply.

Jake Pendleton stepped into the silent house. The kitchen and dining room seemed undisturbed. The living room was a mess. Ransacked, obviously.

Pendleton drew his revolver and motioned to the rookie he was training to do likewise. The two officers moved slowly up the stairs to the second floor and stopped at the door of the largest room.

"Oh, my God!" gasped the rookie.

"Don't make a move, Cecil. Stay perfectly still and don't touch anything."

The woman on the bed was sprawled on her back. Her head was covered by a blood-soaked pillowcase.

"It's Mrs. Vogel, Jake! I've known her ever since I was a little kid!"

"I know, Cecil. But there's nothing we can do for her now. We have to step back out of here now and leave everything for the detectives just the way we've found her."

"She always had cookies and milk for us kids! She did, Jake! Always!"

"That's right, Cecil. But now we have to take a deep breath and then we have to go room to room and make sure there's nobody hiding in the house. Her killer's probably long gone, but stay alert. Just in case, Okay?"

"Yeah, sure, Jake."

"Once we secure the house, we call it in. While we wait for the detectives, we can look around and make notes. But we won't disturb anything. And we won't offer the detectives any advice. Got it? They don't care what we think about anything."

"Yeah, Jake. I got it. But why would anyone want to kill a nice old lady like Mrs. Vogel? She wasn't mean or rich or anything."

"I don't know why either, Cecil. Somebody may figure that out, but it won't be us."

"But it's so horrible, Jake. I can't stop wondering why."

"To tell the truth, Cecil, neither can I. But we'll just keep our theories between us, okay? From here on, we'll just answer the detectives and do what they tell us to do."

THREE DAYS AFTER THE discovery of Mrs. Natasha Vogel's body, Detective Paul Mooney of the Bellefonte Police Department finally found a next of kin to notify. The dead woman's pastor had suggested he call the Catholic Chancery Office in Pittsburgh which referred him to the Jesuit Province's office in Oak Park, Illinois, where a Mrs. Henrietta Leary took his call.

"You've phoned at a bad time," she said. "Father Provincial is on his way to the University of Detroit and can't be reached until tomorrow. But I'll make sure he gets your message when he returns next Monday."

Detective Mooney sighed. "Well, maybe you can help me, ma'am. We want to make sure that we notify one of your priests, a Father Alex Samozvanyetz, that his sister has died."

"Oh, I'm so sorry," said Mrs. Leary.

"She was found murdered at her home here earlier this week."

"Murdered, you say? That's dreadful. Do you know who did it?"

"No, not yet. But we found family records in her house that indicate that this Father Alex Samozvanyetz was Mrs. Vogel's only living relative. So we're trying to get in touch with him."

"Yes, of course. That's very thoughtful of you."

"Do you know where he can be reached?"

"No, not offhand. His name isn't familiar to me. But let me check our files."

Detective Mooney waited patiently until the woman returned to the phone.

"All I can tell you is that he's a missionary, but I don't know where. From what I can see, he left our province to study in Rome back before the war. There's nothing current on him in our files. He may be deceased himself, for all I know. But I'm sure Father Provincial will be able to get a message to him if he's still alive. There aren't that many Jesuits in the world, you know."

"Well, I'd appreciate it if someone could find him and let him know about his sister. I'll be happy to give him a full report if he wants to call me."

He gave the woman his name and telephone number.

"I'll make sure Father Provincial's secretary gets this information. He's very thorough. I'm sure we'll find Father Samozvanyetz and break the news to him that his sister is dead."

"Murdered," said the detective.

"I beg your pardon?"

"I said she was murdered. During a burglary in her home."

"Yes, murdered, of course. Well, God rest her soul, the poor dear. But she's at peace now, I'm sure."

Later that morning, Mrs. Leary placed a note on Brother Al Krause's desk where he would be sure to see it upon his return.

Police Detective Paul Muni in Bellport, Penn, called to inform Father Provincial that Mrs. Natasha Vogel, the sister of Father Alex Samozvanyetz, S.J., died this week there. Father S. is her only known relative. Said you would find Father S. and let him know. Have enrolled Mrs. Vogel in our Perpetual Mass Association.

She signed the note and added the detective's name and telephone number.

The following Monday, the Provincial and his secretary spent the morning disposing of accumulated paperwork.

"About this note from Mrs. Leary," said the Provincial, "I think we'll leave this for Father Beck to deal with when he takes over. He'll know how to handle it much better than I do."

The Provincial put the note to one side.

"What's next?" he said.

EARLIER IN THE SPRING of 1956, Father John Beck, S.J., who taught Latin and Greek at St. Ignatius High School in Cleveland, Ohio, received a letter from the Jesuit Father General in Rome advising him that he was appointed to be the head of the Chicago Province of the Society of Jesus. Father Beck would assume the office of Provincial later that summer and, for the next six years, he would be the superior of all the Jesuit priests, scholastics and lay brothers in Illinois, Indiana, Michigan and Ohio, and would oversee the province's high schools, colleges, universities, churches and houses of study.

Father Beck dropped the letter on his desk and said, "Oh, nuts!" He had never aspired to high office. He did not want the job of Provincial or the authority that went with it. But he had no choice. It was, he said later when his appointment became known, the most severe test of his vow of obedience in all his years as a Jesuit.

"I just hope I can keep my same hat size," he told his fellow Jesuits. The promotion did not seem to go to Father Beck's head. If anything, he became more modest. His colleagues noted only one change in his behavior. Until that June, Father Beck had always read the daily newspapers standing up because, he would say if anyone inquired, "A standing man is less prone to distraction."

Every evening after supper, Father Beck would stand at a table in the priests' recreation room and skim through the *Press*, the *News* and *The Plain Dealer* while the conversations flowed around him. He quickly checked the obituaries, the sports results and the first three paragraphs of all major news stories. He scanned the headlines of the business, real estate and entertainment sections, but ignored most editorials, columns, letters to the editor, food and fashion features, and helpful hints for housewives and handymen.

He did, however, follow the adventures of Li'l Abner, Orphan Annie and Dick Tracy. Once a week, he spent ten minutes paging through *Time* magazine and the *Catholic Universe Bulletin* "to stay abreast of trends in mass culture."

But that June he sat down to read newspaper and

magazine speculation about the speech Nikita Khrushchev may have made in the secret session of the Twentieth
Congress of the Communist Party in Moscow.

The *New York Times* had managed to obtain and print
what it believed was a full text of the Khrushchev speech
and it was reprinted in the Cleveland *Plain Dealer*. Father
Beck studied it carefully. There were a few new details, but
Father Beck had known or suspected what had been happening under Lenin and Stalin since the Russian Revolution.

During the war, he had hoped that Hitler's defeat might
halt Stalin's terror. But, in the Soviet Union, mercy had not
followed victory. He had a surge of hope when Stalin died
in 1952. But the executions continued, the gates of the Soviet prisons remained locked, and exiles continued to suffer and die in Siberia.

Father Beck studied the accounts of Khrushchev's career, just as he had scrutinized his secret speech, wondering
if things would be different in Russia now. "De-Staliniza-
tion" was what the papers were calling Khrushchev's policy. But, as far as Father Beck could see, there was no real
change. Khrushchev's attack on Stalin and what he called
his "cult of personality" was most likely only a bold political stroke by an ambitious politician.

"Business as usual," concluded Father Beck. He put
aside the papers and magazines and wasted no more time
on speculation.

The minutes he saved were spent in the chapel. But

prayer and meditation produced only two good things to say about his new assignment. It was God's will and it was terminal. Jesuit provincials serve for six years. Then they are removed from their position of authority and returned to the ranks.

That can't be soon enough, thought Father Beck.

CHAPTER · 4

IT WAS THE SUMMER of 1961 and Harold Hoffmann was wasting his time in the Soviet Union. It hadn't taken him long to figure that out. He'd gone there with a bunch of Iowa farmers and agricultural professors, ready to give Russian farmers any help he could. Once there, he found that the Soviet government people escorting the American goodwill group didn't want any help.

Harold didn't know exactly what they were: bureaucrats, guides, interpreters, spies maybe. They sure didn't want any advice. Much less any criticism, real or imagined. They didn't know spit about agriculture, but they sure knew their Marx and Lenin. "Our jailers" is how he came to think of them.

Was he the only one in the group who felt strongly about any of this? He guessed he was. The other Americans seemed to be having a good enough time, eating the Russian food, drinking the Russian vodka and taking snapshots of each other visiting Russia. So here he was in Siberia, stuck with a bunch of dumb Americans who didn't seem to give a damn, and being escorted by a squad of Commie bastards who were insulting his intelligence.

The tour guides made him madder than hell with all their denying that anything was going wrong anywhere in their damned country. They even denied what he could plainly see: they were having a drought. Harold was a farmer and farmers know about drought, dammit. Any fool could look at the sky at sunset and see that dark band just above the horizon. That meant that their topsoil was blowing away, for God's sake!

By now, with one more week to go, he had no one to talk to. After a month on this road, Harold's companions had tired of listening to his observations and complaints. Even those who more or less agreed with him felt it best to keep their opinions to themselves. "We're not here to bitch about everything, Harold. We're representing the United States here, don't forget. So be polite, for God's sake!"

And so it was that by the time the Americans reached the seedy hotel somewhere in Siberia, there was only one person willing to listen to what Harold Hoffmann had to say: one of his jailers. Her name was Anya Something. He never could pronounce her last name right, so he'd started calling her "Comrade Anya" and she said that was "Okay" with her. Her English was a hell of a lot better than the rest of the jailers. Almost like an American.

Anya was a real person, not a robot: a yellow-haired young woman with a round face. He figured she was about the same age as his son's wife, maybe younger. But she had old eyes, best as he could describe them. Harold sensed the presence of a wise person behind them, someone reasonable, someone he could talk to. And so he did.

Anya's dark eyes never left his when he spoke with her. He told her how lonely and isolated he felt, and she listened. She listened when he told her how he felt about the banquets and the ordinary Russian folks watching the Americans eat and she nodded. She listened when he told her about the cloud of topsoil along the horizon. And she smiled sadly when he talked about being prevented from seeing the real Russia. Or visiting with the real Russian people.

"Everything seems staged," he said. "Clean, neat, orderly—even the people. I wish I could just get one chance to see what life on a farm here is really like."

"That I can fix," said Anya.

"You could do that?"

"I can take you someplace where you can, is 'wander' the right word, yes? Where you can just wander around and see things for yourself. Stay in bed tomorrow morning when everyone else gets up, Harold. Say you're sick. Too hung over to travel. I'll take care of the rest."

"Won't you get into trouble?"

"Maybe I will and maybe I won't." Anya shrugged and smiled. "We can steal an hour or two away from the others. Depends on how convincing your hangover is."

That next morning, an hour after the bus carrying the Iowa delegation left the Siberian hotel, Harold Hoffmann squeezed himself into the two-door sedan Anya had commandeered. He felt terrible.

"You played your part well last night," Anya said.

"Maybe too well for your own good. I'm sorry for your pain, Harold, but I must say your distress this morning was most believable."

Harold was about to ask how big a fool he had made of himself, but thought better of it. Making conversation would only make things worse. He didn't remember throwing up during the night, but brushing his teeth three times hadn't rid his mouth of the taste of vomit. The hotel's coffee and the aspirins from his shaving kit hadn't stopped the throbbing in his head.

Anya drove on in silence, thank God, her eyes fastened on the narrow strip of pavement that stretched straight out to the horizon. Harold saw no other automobiles on the road, only an occasional truck approaching from the opposite direction. After an hour or so, Anya slowed the car and parked by a stand of white birch trees.

"We've arrived," said Anya. A dirt road angled off to the right, marked by a large white sign with black lettering that Harold couldn't decipher.

Anya sat motionless for a moment with her hands on the steering wheel, staring ahead through the windshield. "I grew up an orphan, Harold. My mother starved to death in Leningrad during the siege. Someone found me and I survived. My brother died fighting the Germans. My father never returned from the war."

Harold started to speak, but she raised her right hand to silence him. "You can't imagine what our war was like, the millions who died. You can't understand our love of country any more than you can comprehend the vastness of our land itself. We're not blind to the problems we face. We're aware of what difficulties we must overcome, what must be changed. We know these things, Harold. We're not children to be scolded and admonished. You have no need to lecture us."

Harold looked out his window. The gray sky and the dark earth seemed infinite. "I'm sorry," he said. "I didn't mean to hurt you, Anya."

She spat out something in Russian, and then turned to face him. "You say we never let you see what you want to see. Well, down that road is a farm. No one there is expecting visitors today. I'll take you there, right now, if you wish. Walk around by yourself, talk to anyone you want, take your pictures. I'll wait in the car."

"You're sure that you won't get into trouble?"

"Don't worry about that. I'll say the car broke down and I went to the farm for help. Somebody may even believe it." She drummed her fingers on the steering wheel. "Well, what's your decision? Go or don't go. Look or don't look. It's completely up to you."

"Okay," Harold said. It didn't seem like too big a deal. "Let's go see what's down that road."

"Okay," said Anya. "But remember the time, Harold. We can't stay too long."

The state farm, when they reached it, looked like all the others he had passed through, cut from the same official pattern. But this one hadn't been spruced up, that was for sure. Alone at last, Harold Hoffmann meandered along dirt lanes that ran past wooden barns and sheds. This, he figured, was what was left of the village that was here before the Communists took over the country and collectivized the farms.

There weren't many people about at this hour. Most were out in the fields, he supposed. He nodded to the few men and women he passed. They stared at him, and kept staring, but they didn't respond to his friendly nods. He smiled at the children. They smiled back but kept their distance. He took some snapshots: a horse and wagon creaking by, a few weathered log houses with decorated window frames, a row of weary grey concrete apartment buildings beyond the fields.

Harold approached a small group of people and held out his camera. "You folks mind if I take your picture?" he said. The people stared at him in silence. "Amerikansky!" he explained. An old man in a military cap waved him off and walked away scowling. A woman in a headscarf with a small boy in short pants smiled and struck a pose. He snapped their picture and walked on.

Harold saw two trucks and a dismantled tractor parked next to a wooden shed. Shafts of sunlight from cracks in the roof slanted down on the mechanic and the vehicle he was repairing. Harold walked inside.

"I wonder if you'd let me take your picture," he said, holding out his camera. "Amerikansky."

Without looking up, the man murmured, "So am I."

The mechanic's lips barely moved. Harold had to strain to hear him.

"Become deeply interested in my work," said the man. "We're being watched, without a doubt. Don't get me in more trouble than I'm in already."

The mechanic glanced up at him.

"That's good," the man said. "Keep that poker face."

"Jesus Christ!" Harold whispered. "You're an American!"

"Yes, but don't get excited. Stay calm. I need your help desperately. You can walk away right now and I wouldn't blame you. But I beg you to help me."

Harold stuffed down the urge to flee and spoke in a loud voice. "I'm sure sorry you don't understand English, mister." Whoever was watching would hear every word. "It sure looks like you could use some help. That's going to be damn hard to fix."

The mechanic looked up, bewildered. He said something in Russian, laughed and shrugged, then looked under the hood of the truck again. "Thank God you're going to help," he said through his teeth. "Just remember: we're two men who don't understand each other's language, one man helping another, concentrating on what we're doing. Do as I tell you and we'll be safe. I want you to take a letter and hand it to someone back home. Only that one person. He's the only one who can help me. No time to explain more than that."

Harold moved the mechanic aside and peered at the tractor engine. "Let's get on with it," he said.

"God bless you," murmured the mechanic. "Listen carefully."

For the next few minutes, Harold fiddled with the engine and concentrated hard on what the mechanic was telling him. The letter was inside a toolbox. The box was on a workbench by the wall to his right. Go to the bench to get a pair of pliers. Stand with back to door. Open the toolbox, lift out the metal tray that sits above tools. Lift with left hand. Support lid with right hand on bottom of tray. Keeping right elbow steady, bend over and look for pliers. Right hand fingers feel for envelope stuck to bottom of tray. Peel it off; slip it into shirt without moving right elbow. Pick up pliers, replace tray, close lid, return to the truck. "If that's clear, scratch your nose." Harold did so. "You can do it if you concentrate and keep breathing," said the mechanic.

Harold grabbed the wrench from the man's hand, thrust it at the tractor engine, unthreaded a nut from a bolt and held it up. "See that?" he said. "There's your damn problem. So now, let's solve it!"

The mechanic grinned, nodded his head, took back his wrench and addressed the tractor engine. "First, we get your two middle shirt buttons undone. Watch me. My work has begun to baffle you. You don't like what I'm doing, so step back slightly. Your belly begins to itch. You're barely aware of it, but you start scratching with your right hand fingers. What's this crazy Russian doing? The fingers of your right hand undo those buttons, slow and gentle. But now you're more upset. You're so frustrated, you're going to snatch the wrench and show me how an American gets the job done. Now do it!"

Harold went through the motions, stepping back, unbuttoning his shirt, grabbing the wrench, banging it on the engine. The mechanic berated him in Russian, and then leaned closer to the engine.

"We're ready to get the letter," he muttered. "Take some deep breaths, very slowly. Let your body relax. You've got all the time in the world. Move slowly. Don't force your movements. You're not frightened. You're playing a game. It's fun. Keep breathing. Stay alert. We now begin."

Suddenly, the mechanic howled in pain. Harold gasped and dropped the wrench. The mechanic jumped away from the truck. He shook his left hand up and down. He doubled over, holding his hand, cursing in Russian. Harold couldn't help laughing. The mechanic glared at him, gasped for air and began laughing, too. He babbled away in Russian, gesturing at the truck, showing Harold his hand, shrugging, grimacing, laughing, cursing.

"Slow down, old buddy!" Harold grasped the man by the shoulders. "I don't know what you're saying, but I know it hurts. Let me take a look." The mechanic let him inspect his hand. "Don't look too bad," said Harold. The mechanic pulled his hand back. He snarled and kicked the dirt floor. He sighed and shook his head. Then he pointed to the toolbox on the workbench by the wall of the shed. He chattered away in Russian, rapidly moving his fists in front of his body. First together, then apart, together and apart, again and again.

Harold took a moment to decipher the gesture: the mechanic was opening and closing an enormous pair of pliers. "Okay," Harold said out loud. "I got it." He opened and closed his own imaginary pliers and pointed to the toolbox. "You want a pair of pliers?"

"*Da, da, da,*" said the mechanic. Both men laughed and Harold started walking across the oily dirt floor. Halfway to the workbench, he saw the balance of sunlight and shadow change. He glanced around. Something was blocking the light from the doorway of the shed. It was Anya, dammit!

"Be with you in a minute," he called to her and kept moving.

"Can't you hurry? It's getting late. We have to catch up with the others."

"I'll only be a minute! Just giving this guy some help. We're just about finished." Anya started to walk toward him and Harold held up his hand. "Don't come in! The floor's awful dirty. You'll ruin your shoes with all the oil and grease around. I won't be but a minute or two longer, honest."

Anya looked down at the dirt floor and stopped. But she stayed in the doorway. Harold got to the table. He took another deep breath and made sure his body blocked Anya's view. Then he finished doing what the mechanic had told him to do. Had his elbow moved? He couldn't tell. But the envelope was inside his shirt. He reached inside the toolbox, took out the pliers, turned and held them up. "This what you want?" he called out. "*Da, da, da,*" said the mechanic and waved him back to the truck.

Harold handed him the pliers. "I got the letter okay," Harold whispered, "but that's my guide at the door." The mechanic didn't look up. "Then let's push on," he said. "Get your shirt buttoned. I'm going to want an American cigarette. And you'll want to take my picture. The picture's important. Make sure you deliver it with the letter."

"Harold!" Anya called out. "We really must hurry!"

"She's coming in," said the mechanic. "No time to rehearse. Let's just do it."

"There will be trouble if we don't get started," Anya called out. She was getting closer to the truck.

"Okay, okay," said Harold over his shoulder. He got his last shirt button secured just as Anya got to him. The mechanic stepped back from the truck, wiped his hands with a rag, bowed to Anya and began talking to her in Russian.

"He says he thanks you for your help," said Anya. "He says you know a lot about tractors and he's sorry you don't understand Russian. He'd really like an American cigarette, and I say we'll get out of here a lot faster if you give him the whole damned package."

"Ask him if I can take his picture."

"Harold! Please, no more delay! We have to go!"

"Come on, it'll just take a minute. Something to remember him by. Here, I'm giving him my cigarettes. Tell him I think he's a nice guy, I liked working with him, and I want to take his picture."

Anya scowled at Harold, but translated his words. The mechanic took the pack of cigarettes, bowed and spoke to Harold in Russian. "He says he's honored to accept your gift," Anya said, "and he'd be even more honored to have you take his photograph."

Harold adjusted his camera. The man struck a pose by his disabled truck, arms folded across his chest, his chin raised high. Harold clicked the shutter.

"There, you have it," said Anya. "You have your picture."

"Just one more! I think I moved. One more to be safe."

This time he remembered to hold his breath and to keep his elbows tight against his body. This time the camera did not shake. "Got it," he said. He suddenly realized that his head wasn't aching anymore.

Anya took his arm and hustled him out of the shed and back to their automobile.

"So now you know that Russian trucks break down and have to be repaired," she said as she bumped the car up the dirt road back to the paved highway. "You've discovered our dark secret. At long last, you've seen something terrible that we didn't want you to see." Anya kept her eyes on the road. "At least you got your hands and shirt dirty," she said. "It will make my story more convincing. We had a break-down and you were able to fix the car's motor."

"With what? My bare hands?"

"There's a tool kit in the boot. That's what you used. I

have no idea of what went wrong or how you fixed it. Can you think of anything else that will make sense?"

"Not really," Harold said.

They were back on pavement now. The envelope kept shifting under Harold's shirt. It felt enormous. His head began to throb again. What the hell had he got himself into?

It took another anxious hour to catch up with the delegation at the next hotel. The Iowans and their escorts were getting ready for their evening meal. There were questions and expressions of concern. Harold lied convincingly, he thought. The Americans seemed to believe his story; the Russian guides didn't react at all.

When Harold returned from his room after washing up and changing his shirt, he saw Anya standing with two men who wore double-breasted suits. He hadn't seen them before and it worried him that the men didn't take their hats off while talking to her. After a few minutes of conversation, they ushered her from the lobby and down a corridor to another room, probably an office.

Anya looked back at him over her shoulder as she walked through the doorway. At that distance, Harold couldn't tell if she was frightened or not. But he sure as hell was.

Would Anya be returning to the tour group? The Russian escorts said nothing about her absence. They behaved as if she had never been there to begin with. Was there anything he could do? He was afraid to ask any questions. If

Anya was in trouble, all he could do was make it worse for her. The rush of excitement Harold had felt in the mechanic's shed was long gone.

He had the mechanic's letter in his pocket and the roll of exposed film as well. He could destroy them, of course. But he couldn't do that. He couldn't think of anything to do but keep quiet and keep going. But very carefully. The Russian escorts had stopped smiling and were having trouble understanding English.

Next morning at breakfast, one of them announced that the Iowans' tour had come to an end. Fortunately, he said, the American visitors had been to all the places of any importance. That wasn't true, Harold knew, but no one from Iowa seemed eager to argue the point. All of them had seen more than enough of the Soviet Union and were happy to go home, none more so than Harold Hoffmann.

But he remained full of fear and worry for Anya and for himself all the way out of Siberia and back to the airport on the outskirts of Moscow. Arrangements had been made for an Aeroflot plane to carry the Americans out of the Soviet Union back to the West. But first, Harold would have to get the mechanic's letter and his undeveloped photo through Soviet Customs.

It had been easy getting behind the Iron Curtain: all welcoming smiles and no red tape. But now the security guards and customs inspectors at the Moscow airport were grim and meticulous. A tall, unsmiling man in a brown military uniform took his own sweet time rummaging through Harold's luggage. He felt around underneath Harold's clothes, checked his shaving kit, examined his camera and his yellow plastic cans of exposed 35mm film. Was he from Customs or the KGB? Would Harold himself be searched? He had the can of film with the mechanic's picture and his letter hidden in the pouch of his Jockey shorts. Harold concentrated on breathing normally, trying not to look guilty.

The Customs inspector stopped what he was doing. He stared coldly at Harold for at least a full minute. Then, without a word or a nod, he closed Harold's suitcases and waved him off to the departure gates. It took Harold several paces before he felt confident enough to take a deep breath.

It was a long, uncomfortable journey from Moscow to the West. Not until he reached the stall of the lavatory of the Air France terminal in Paris did he dare transfer the film canister and the letter from his shorts to his jacket pocket.

CHAPTER · 5

A WEEK OF HEAT and humidity had been oppressing Chicago and Father John Beck could feel the approach of summer's last great storm. He stood gazing out his office window watching the leaves of the maple trees turn silver in the yellowish green light. The garden behind the mansion, which now served as the Jesuit Provincial's office and residence, had fallen silent. The birds and squirrels had gone to those secret places where they find refuge in times of danger. Father Beck wondered aloud where they went.

Brother Alphonse Krause, the Provincial's secretary, said he had no idea.

"You could ask your visitor when he gets here, Father. I think he might be a farmer."

"Did he say he was a farmer, Brother Al?"

"No, I just assumed he was. He was calling from Iowa."

"Well, farmer or not, I hope he gets here before the storm hits. Anybody left in the offices?"

"No, I told everybody to leave. They should be safe at home by now. And I've made sure all the windows are closed."

"Good," said Father Beck. "Nothing to do now but wait."

WELL, I'M USED TO *waiting,* thought Father Beck. It had been a long five and a half years, waiting for his term as Provincial to end. His successor would be chosen before the year was out and he'd be moving on to become Master of Novices at the Novitiate of the Sacred Heart at Milford, Ohio, near Cincinnati. That's what he'd been told, and that was fine with him. He hadn't enjoyed having so much authority over his fellow Jesuits.

But today was today. He was still Provincial and a man was driving all the way from Iowa to tell him something he said was important. Brother Al had taken the long distance telephone call earlier in the week.

"I'm a Methodist," the man had said, "so I don't know exactly how to go about this." He wouldn't say why he wanted to speak with the Jesuit Provincial face-to-face, but he insisted it was urgent. Brother Al said he thought the man sounded frightened, or very nervous, anyway. So he made the appointment. And now Harold Hoffmann was due to arrive in an hour.

"We ought to change before our Methodist farmer gets here, Brother Al. It's probably better not to greet our visitor in our cassocks, especially if he's frightened about something. You'll look less threatening in a shirt and tie."

Father Beck walked down the hall past the empty

clerical offices, across the mansion's large foyer, up the wide, curving staircase to the second floor, then along the carpeted corridor that led to his living quarters. Turn the lights off on the way down, he told himself. No sense wasting electricity. He made sure his bedroom windows were closed before hanging his cassock in his closet.

His bathroom was still damp from his morning shower. He washed his hands and face, then pressed the cold washcloth against his eyes and held it there. Harold the herald: what problem does this anxious messenger bring? And why is he so troubled? Most likely, it has to do with something personal. But why come here? Why not find help closer to home in his own church?

Father Beck slipped into a short-sleeved black shirt with a Roman collar. He checked his appearance in the mirror above his dresser. He didn't look Methodist, but he might pass for Episcopalian. That would have to do.

HAROLD HOFFMANN HAD BEEN watching the clouds building up over the Great Plains ever since making his call to Chicago and he knew that the gathering storm would be powerful and full of damage. His son had urged him to delay his trip until the storm passed, but Harold had shaken off his objections and left that morning at dawn. He kept his big blue Oldsmobile cruising a safe ten miles over the limit and managed to stay ahead of the storm. He lost time locating the address in the unfamiliar northern suburbs of Chicago, so the light was almost gone when he finally turned a corner in Oak Park and parked his car across from an old mansion on a large corner lot. It was set well back from both streets. In the fading light, the building and the old trees on the property looked downright spooky.

Harold put on his steel-rimmed reading glasses and checked the directions he'd jotted down in his notebook. He'd found the right place, thank God. He snapped open the glove compartment, shoved aside the flashlight and road maps, worked the felt lining loose and withdrew a manila envelope he'd taped to the top of the metal frame. He shook off a sudden recollection of the Siberian mechanic's toolbox. He felt like throwing up. But he tucked the envelope into his jacket pocket and tried to calm down.

A fat raindrop splattered on his windshield. Then another and another. He'd better hurry. Harold clambered out of his Oldsmobile, slammed the car door shut, and galloped across the street. There was an overhead light in the portico covering the mansion's side entrance and Harold ran toward it. Just as he got there, a powerful gust of wind shoved him sideways against the thick wooden door. Harold Hoffmann and the storm had reached the Provincial's residence at precisely the same moment.

Lightning slashed away the darkness. Hard rain crashed down. Thunder boomed. The door swung open as Harold lunged through the doorway and cried out, "Jesus Christ Almighty!"

"Amen," said the doorkeeper. Harold saw the short-sleeved black shirt and the Catholic priest-collar and stammered out an apology.

The man in black laughed and waved him off.

A sudden gust swept a thick curtain of rain up the driveway and Harold helped shoulder the heavy door shut.

"Well, that's got it," said the priest. "You didn't get here a minute too soon, Mr. Hoffmann. I must say I've never had a visitor arrive with such fanfare before."

"Yeah, I thought that lightning had got me for sure," said Harold. "Are you Father Provincial?"

"I am, but that's my job title." He shook Harold's hand. "My name's John Beck. Come along to my office where that storm can't get at us. You can just call me John, by the way."

Harold looked around the large entry hall. At the far end, a wide staircase wound up through the gloom to the floor above. "Some place you got here," he said.

"Yes, it's big and gloomy, isn't it? But it's not haunted. A wealthy couple left it to us when they died, but they haven't come back to visit, thank goodness. Just as well: I'm sure they'd be appalled at how we've converted their palace from luxurious to functional. As you can see, it's a bit of both."

Harold followed the priest down a dimly lit corridor past several dark offices with nobody in them. "The mansion would've made a nice museum or an art gallery, but we turned it into an administrative headquarters. Actually, I've spent most of my term trying to unload this place."

He stopped and peered at Harold. "You wouldn't be in the market, would you? No, I didn't think so. Too much to hope for, I guess."

Was the priest kidding him? Harold wasn't sure.

"That's the trouble with accumulating worldly possessions," said the priest as he continued walking. "They're too darn hard to get rid of."

He ushered Harold into a large wood-paneled room and introduced him to Brother Al Krause, a younger man with a firm handshake, about the same size as he was, but leaner. Black shoes, black trousers, white shirt, black tie. Harold thought he looked like a security guard or maybe a real cop.

Turned out he was the Father Provincial's private secretary. He was a Jesuit, too, but he wasn't a priest. He was a "lay brother." The priests did the religious business, Harold learned, like saying the Mass and hearing confessions. The brothers took care of the non-religious stuff.

"Like stoking the furnace and fixing the plumbing," Al Krause said with a smile. "And also handling mail and phone calls for the Boss."

For Harold, it was all strange and confusing. But the coffee was strong and the furniture was comfortable, even if it did look out of place in a rich man's house. John and Al seemed like nice enough guys and they were sure doing their darndest to put him at ease. So he settled back into the leather armchair and relaxed.

The floor lamps were lit, not the overheads, so the room

was dark around the edges. After a few minutes of small talk about his long drive and the storm, John Beck, sitting on the leather sofa across from him, spoke softly, "How may we help you, Harold?"

"This is real hard for me, John. I don't know where to start."

"The beginning is usually a good place," said the priest. "Take all the time you want. We don't have anything else to do this evening. We'll fix something to eat later and you can spend the night here, if you wish. We get a lot of visitors, so we have plenty of guest rooms." The priest leaned back in the sofa. "You wouldn't mind if Brother Al takes some notes, would you?"

Harold didn't mind at all. He took another swallow of coffee and waited until the brother had seated himself at the desk in front of the big picture window.

Thunder was still rumbling outside the old mansion and rain slashed across the glass. Harold got off to a slow start but he managed to tell his whole story, from the beginning of his tour of the Soviet Union to its end here in the Provincial's office in Oak Park.

"When I finally got home to Iowa," Harold concluded, "I was still scared. Couldn't get over the feeling I was being watched all the time. Still can't. Anyhow, before I went back to the farm, I got my photos developed in a shop in Des Moines. It's a pretty big city and I figured nobody would pay much attention to the pictures in Des Moines, or to me either. Took me a while to figure out how to get in touch with you, but I didn't want to call until I went back to pick up the pictures in Des Moines and made sure they came out okay. Then I called from a pay phone there to ask to see you. And here I am."

Harold took the manila envelope from his jacket pocket. "Everything's in there," he said. "The letter's inside another envelope I picked up at that hotel in Siberia. I stuck it in there because I didn't want to touch his letter any more than I had to. I was tempted a few times, but I never opened it. It's your business, not mine. The pictures of the man I met are in the envelope from the photo shop. They're the only prints I had made and I'm giving you the negatives."

Leaning forward, Harold handed the manila envelope to Father Beck. "I just hope my part in this is over and done with and I can put all this behind me."

Father Beck turned the envelope over in his hands, but did not open it.

"You're a kind, brave man, Harold. You remind me of the Good Samaritan in the parable. You found a stranger in great distress and did everything you could to help him get to safety. I hope we'll be able to continue your good work. We'll do everything we can to help him as well. Just leave everything in our hands."

Brother Krause got to his feet and came around the desk to Harold's chair.

"Why don't you and I go out to the kitchen, Harold? We'll have a beer and rustle up some sandwiches. We'll have Father Beck join us when they're ready."

"That's a deal, Al. I'm sure glad you aren't Baptists. I could sure use a beer after all that."

ALONE IN HIS OFFICE, Father Beck opened the manila envelope and emptied its contents onto his desk. Inside the Siberian hotel envelope he found the smaller one. It was faded, discolored, smudged with dirt and grease. Father Beck thought he could make out a couple of fingerprints. The address was printed in pencil:

> Jesuit Provincial
> Chicago Province
> Chicago, Illinois, U.S.A.

"Nice work finding me, Mr. Hoffmann," Father Beck said to himself. "Not much for a Methodist to go on."

He opened the flap of the yellow envelope and let the photographs slip out. There were more than a dozen pictures: a couple of group shots of the American farmers and their tour guides and more than a dozen photos of the state farm and the Russian people who lived and worked there. Father Beck isolated the two photos he wanted to study.

One was slightly blurred. The other was in sharp focus. He could see the interior of the barn was exactly as Hoffmann had described: the workbench, the old truck, the shafts of sunlight. The rest was in shadow. But there, posing proudly beside the cab of the truck was Alex Samozvanyetz! No doubt about it!

His hair was grey, his face lined and weather-beaten. But there was no mistaking his smile and those dark eyes.

Father Beck buried his face in his hands and thanked God that his friend was still alive. He had prayed for Alex every day for two decades: first for his health and safety and then, as years of silence wore on, for the repose of his soul. But there stood Alex, chin up and undefeated, as if risen from the grave.

Father Beck wiped his eyes with his handkerchief and blew his nose. Carefully, he slit open the smaller envelope and extracted the folded sheet of paper. In the upper left corner were the initials *AMDG*—the abbreviated motto of the Society of Jesus *ad majorem Dei gloriam* for the greater glory of God.

> Reverend Father,
>
> *Christi.* I pray I am not forgotten. My sentence has been served and I am living on parole where the bearer of this letter found me. People here don't know my true identity. The authorities do. My health is good. I work and pray. I wait for what comes next. God's will be done. Please pray for your brother in Christ,
>
> Alex Samozvanyetz, S.J.

Father Beck reached for his Breviary and extracted the faded letter he touched every time he read his Daily Office. It was a letter from Rome, the last he had received from Alex more than twenty years ago.

He placed it beside the letter from Russia and compared

the handwriting: old and new, young and old, but obviously the same hand. Slowly, he walked to the center of the room and stood with his hands clasped and contemplated the wooden crucifix on the wall.

God is good, he thought. How miraculous that he was the Provincial who received this good news. He had only a few months of authority left, but that might be time enough to bring his friend home from captivity. Or, at least, get the process started. That, he knew, would take more than prayer.

He returned to his desk to jot down his first thoughts about the letter he would send to the Father General in Rome. What struck him immediately was that he was handing his superior a very hot potato. And that it was vital that the Iowa farmer tell no one about his encounter with the American Jesuit in Siberia.

He capped his fountain pen and hurried to the kitchen to join Brother Al and Harold Hoffmann. As it turned out, Hoffmann needed no explanations or any persuasion.

"I made up my mind straight off. I wasn't going to talk about him to any reporters or friends or even my son and daughter-in-law. I know the man's in deep trouble and I'm not about to do anything to put his life in danger. His secret's safe with me, so help me God!"

All Harold Hoffmann wanted was to get back home. But he was more than willing to spend the night in the Provincial's residence. "Fact is, I don't want to spend the night alone in some motel tonight. I'm still not over being scared to death."

Harold Hoffmann left Oak Park right after breakfast and drove home under a clear blue sky, darned glad that his errand was over and done with.

FATHER BECK'S LETTER TO the Father General ran six pages in English. He'd started translating it into Latin while Brother Al was attacking his regular clerical chores in the outer office, clearing his desk for the morning's typing job.

"I'm just about finished," said Father Beck when Brother Al announced that he was ready to begin. "Here's a few pages to get you started. I hope it's not too difficult. It's in Latin, you know."

Brother Krause shrugged. "Latin, English: it's all Greek to me, Father. I just type it one letter at a time."

He went to his desk in the outer office, hunched over his typewriter and began tapping out what Father Beck knew would be a clean copy of a long letter written in a language this husky man with quick fingers couldn't understand.

It was a good letter, Father Beck had to admit as he began proofreading the pages Brother Krause produced. Precise as to detail, Ciceronian in style, the letter's graceful periodic sentences presented the facts at hand, considered the political implications for Rome as well as Washington and would close with a suggested course of action that could be taken—with the permission of the Father General, of course.

Father Beck went to the outer office and picked up another page from his secretary's desk. "You know," he said, "you really ought to learn Latin yourself, Brother Al. You type it so accurately. I haven't found a single error so far. That's quite extraordinary."

"Better wait, Father. I'm not finished yet," said Brother Krause. The fingers of his strong hands kept moving.

Father Beck grinned. "Not a bad letter, at all," he said, testing his secretary's concentration. "The vocabulary of the ancient Roman Empire utilized in the 20th Century with no need for circumlocution. Too bad our high school freshmen will never see this epistle and realize that Latin, which most Americans presume to be dead, is alive and well and working *ad majorem Dei gloriam.*"

Brother Krause didn't even look up. The letter was cabled to Rome half an hour later.

FATHER BECK WAS REMINDED, once again, that he didn't have the patience of a saint or anything close to it. He spent the next day stewing about the distance between Chicago and Rome, between himself and the Father General, not to mention the Holy Father. He tried to tell himself that it was unrealistic to expect a rapid reply. But a cablegram from Rome arrived the morning of the second day. One word in English: "Proceed."

Father Beck immediately made two phone calls: one to alert the rector of the Jesuit community at St. Ignatius

High School that he would need a room for the night; the second to schedule an appointment at the Cleveland office of the FBI. While he was packing a small suitcase for his overnight trip, Brother Krause pulled some strings and secured a reservation for his boss on a flight to Cleveland departing at 2:00 p.m. He backed the house car out of the garage and sped Father Beck to O'Hare Airport, getting him there in plenty of time to catch his plane.

LATER THAT NIGHT, BROTHER Krause prowled the Provincial's office bookshelves and pulled out *Latin Grammar for High Schools* by Robert J. Henle, S.J. The book was only 244 pages long. If he could master a page a day, he could finish it in about eight months. Well, why not? He took Henle's grammar upstairs to his room.

He glanced at the small organization chart he had drawn when he first arrived at the Provincial's office. It was pinned to a bulletin board on the bedroom wall along with some notes to himself, a calendar and a poem about St. Alphonse Rodriguez, S.J., which Father Beck had given him on his patron saint's feast day.

At the bottom of his handmade organization chart, Brother Krause had printed Secretary, drawn a line up to Father Provincial, another line up to Father General, another up to Holy Father and a final line up to God. This chain-of-command diagram accurately depicted how Brother Alphonse Krause, S.J., viewed his Jesuit vow of obedience. God's will for him was revealed to him through the orders of his superiors.

It was true that he had not been given a direct order to learn Latin. But behind Father Beck's off-hand remark, Brother Krause had detected the will of his superior, which, he believed, his vow of obedience obliged him to ascertain and follow.

So, with complete willingness and an open mind, Brother Krause turned to the first page of Henle's grammar and learned that the Latin alphabet has no "w" or "y." Otherwise, it is the same as the English alphabet. That was something he had not known before. A new fact, with more to come. Maybe teaching himself Latin wouldn't be too tough a job after all.

CHAPTER · 6

THE FIRST CLASSES OF the morning were starting at Saint Ignatius High School where Father Beck had spent the night. Briefcase in hand, he stepped down the cloister's wooden staircase, stopped, checked his watch, and saw that he had some time to spare. So he turned and climbed all the way up to the fourth floor.

Through the doors which separated the Jesuit living quarters from the high school classrooms, he could hear the freshmen chanting: "*Lau-DO, lau-DAS, lau-DAT! Lau-DAMUS, lau-DATIS, lau-DANT!*"

He took a deep breath and started back down the worn steps, savoring the sounds from the classrooms: Caesar and Homer, Cicero and Virgil, the words of the ancients and the voices of male adolescents growing deeper as he descended past the sophomores to the juniors and the seniors.

He had spent the three years of his Regency teaching here. He was Mister Beck then, one of a dozen scholastics assigned to Ignatius, none of them much older than the lads they taught. During this break from their studies for the priesthood, the scholastics wore cassocks and Roman collars just like the priests on the faculty. But the boys knew the difference. When he returned to teach here several years after ordination, he learned firsthand that teenaged boys were less comfortable with "Father" than they had been with "Mister" Beck.

Times change, he thought. People change and buildings change, too. Heraclitus was right about that. No teacher walks through the same high school twice. The Rector had given him a tour of the building the night before and Father Beck politely noted all the changes since his departure six years before. He didn't mention that some changes made him sad. But the Rector was right, of course. The building was structurally sound, but it did need substantial renovation. The nighttime tour had convinced him of that.

Still, he wished the old school could remain as it always had been. How much tradition, he wondered, would survive the trauma of modernization? Not much, he feared. But the matter was out of his hands. The new Provincial would make the final decisions about the renovation of Saint Ignatius High School. Not John Beck, thank God.

Later that night, before retiring, he had returned by himself to the main hall on the first floor. So far, progress had yet to reach this windowless, high-ceilinged, wainscoted corridor. Without looking, he found the switch on the wall and turned on the overhead lights. They still did little to brighten the hallway, but they cast enough light to see the graduating class photographs on the walls, dating back to the 1890s. He stopped when he reached Mister Beck's classes, recalling all of his boys by name. In most cases, he knew what they had become as men.

He stood for a while regarding the youngster in the middle of the second row of graduates: Herbert Coogan, the first boy in his freshman class to attempt a moustache.

"You'd better shave it off, Herbert," he remembered telling him. "Makes you look like Pancho Villa's kid brother." Young Coogan did get rid of his moustache, but his nickname stuck thanks to a classmate who heard Mister Beck's remark and passed it on to his pals.

The boy in the picture was the man he'd be seeing in the morning. God willing, Pancho Coogan might help him bring Alex Samozvanyetz home from Russia. Father Beck switched off the main hall lights and returned to his room.

THE SKY WAS CLEAR the next day when Father Beck left the high school, walked a block to Bridge Avenue and caught one of the buses that had replaced the old streetcars. It was a short ride across the High Level Bridge to Public Square and then just a brisk walk to his destination.

Twenty-two people, none of whom he recognized, greeted him along the way. "Good morning, Father." "Morning, Father." He picked up two more as he spun through the revolving door of the Federal Building and walked across the lobby. The elevator operator, who stood staring off into space, said: "Good morning, Father." That made it twenty-five.

It took a moment for Father Beck to realize that the man was blind. "If you don't mind my asking," he said as the car ascended, "how did you know that I'm a priest?"

"I have ears, Father," said the blind man. "I can always tell if it's a priest walking up to my elevator."

"Well, I'll be darned," said Father Beck. "Thanks for the ride. I'll keep you in my prayers."

He walked, a bit self-consciously along the corridor to the translucent glass door of the Cleveland office of the Federal Bureau of Investigation. He opened it and walked in.

"Good morning, Father," the receptionist said brightly. Father Beck chuckled. Twenty-six broke his Going-Downtown record. But, before he could introduce himself, the young woman picked up her phone, buzzed an extension and said, "He's here, Agent Coogan."

She smiled at Father Beck. "He'll be here in just a moment, Father. He's really eager to see you."

Special Agent in Charge Herbert Coogan appeared, beaming with pleasure, and paraded his high schoolteacher through a large general office.

"So, you're the boss of all this, are you?" said Father Beck after he nodded and smiled his way through the desks. "I've never seen real G-men in their headquarters before. Not like the movies, is it? More like an accounting firm and your men remind me of the fellows who show up at our class reunions."

"A lot of them do," said Coogan.

After introducing his old teacher to his secretary, he ushered Father Beck into his private office and closed the door which displayed his old student's name and title on it.

"No nickname, I see," said Father Beck. "So how do you like being the man in charge, Herb?"

"About as much as you like being Provincial, Father Beck."

"Actually, I'm just about done with it, thank goodness. I'll be going on to Milford in a few months. If your son stays on course, I'll be his Master of Novices."

"That's great, Father."

"You don't look overjoyed about it."

"Well, it makes me feel better to know that you'll be there. But, honestly, I don't feel right about Charley's decision. I think he's making a mistake. I could be wrong about that, I guess."

"No, you may be right. But we won't keep him if he's not supposed to be there. That's what the novitiate is all about, Herb. It gives young men two years to decide if it's the life for them or not before they commit to it."

"I know," said Coogan. "Anyhow, I've been keeping my thoughts to myself. If he wants to give it a try, I'm not going to do anything to stop him."

"That's a wise decision, Herb. I'll make sure no harm comes to him." Father Beck paused. "Herb," he said, "I had better tell you this straight off that I'm not here to discuss your son's vocation, important though that may be. I'm here because I need your help."

"Well, sure, Father. I'll do anything I can for you. You know that."

"Careful, Herb. This isn't your old pal Mister Beck sitting here. I'm a Jesuit Provincial and I'm here on official business, authorized by the Jesuit Father General in Rome himself."

Herb Coogan said nothing as he studied Father Beck's face for a long moment. He picked up his telephone and buzzed his secretary.

"Give all my calls to Agent Webster," he said. "And tell him I don't want to be disturbed unless it's a real emergency."

He cradled the phone. "She probably thinks you're hearing my confession."

"It's just as serious."

"So I gather," said Coogan. "Does this involve a crime, Father? Or national security?"

"I don't think so."

"You don't know? Or you're not sure?"

"I'm not a lawyer, Herb. I believe it doesn't involve a crime. I'm not sure about national security. It may cause problems for our government, maybe. Should I continue?"

Coogan nodded.

"We have learned that one of our men, an American Jesuit priest, is being held in the Soviet Union. We want to get him out."

Herb Coogan drummed his fingers on his desktop and took a deep breath. "I guess he wasn't snatched off a tourist bus or anything simple like that," he said. "So, how long has he been there?"

"Since some time in 1939, I think. Right around the start of the war in Europe."

"Do you know what he was doing there?"

"Yes, I do. But the Father General would rather I not say too much about that."

"But you want to get him out of the Soviet Union? That's hostile territory, Father. Can't the Vatican get him out?"

"It's hostile territory for the Vatican, too, Herb. I've been tasked to find out, informally, what our government might be able do for him."

Coogan looked up at the portrait of J. Edgar Hoover on his office wall.

"The government will want to know everything there is to know. Holding back facts would be a waste of time and energy, Father. Besides, the Russians probably know everything there is to know about your man by now. They can hang his dirty laundry out on the line anytime it suits their purposes."

"I suppose you're right about all that," said Father Beck. "The best we can hope for, I guess, is a little discretion."

He opened his briefcase and took out a manila file folder.

"I'll give you these copies of everything I've found in our files. There wasn't much about him and nothing has been added since he left the country to study in Rome before the war. You'll find a handwritten letter from Rome he sent me in 1939. It was the last letter I ever received from him. I didn't get many before that and I'm sorry I didn't save any of the others."

Coogan pushed the folder aside.

"Just tell me what you can, Father. Informally."

"Don't you want to bring in a stenographer?"

"Right now, this is just between the two of us."

"Off the record?" said Father Beck. "That certainly makes it a lot easier. Well, what this is all about, really, is the Russian Mission. Have you ever heard of it, Herb? I didn't think so. Not many people have, not even a lot of Jesuits.

"I first heard about it when I was a novice, just starting out. But before I get into that, let me tell you what I know about our man in Russia.

"Father Alex Samozvanyetz was a classmate of mine. His parents were born in Russia. Their families came here before the First World War and the Russian Revolution. Alex's parents met in Detroit and were married rather late in life.

"I met them when they came to visit the novitiate. They were older than the other parents and they didn't speak English very well. Alex had two sisters, both deceased now. One was married with no children; the other was a Poor Clare nun. The family was quite religious, tightly knit, and spoke Russian at home while Alex was growing up, so Russian was his first language. He wasn't much influenced by secular America. Culturally, he was pretty darn Russian when I met him."

"So he has no living relatives," said Coogan.

"Not that I know of. Maybe some distant ones, but I don't recall him mentioning any uncles or cousins."

"Okay," said Coogan. "Tell me what you know about this Russian Mission and how your friend got involved in it."

"I was sitting right next to Alex when I first heard about the Russian Mission. Our Master of Novices was talking to our class about obedience and self-sacrifice. To make a point, he read a letter from the late Pope Pius XI, a call for volunteers the Pope had sent out before any of us entered the Society. I remember that it began: 'To all seminarians, especially our Jesuit sons.'

"The Holy Father described all the religious persecution going on in Russia during the Communist Revolution and said that, one day, the Church would need priests to go to Russia to take the place of those who had been martyred. He was calling for volunteers to enter a special seminary in Rome to prepare for that day.

"I glanced at Alex and I saw a young man transfixed. He seemed unaware of anything else. I wasn't able to speak to him until after the evening meal during the recreation period. All the novices were chattering about the Russian Mission. You know how young men get stirred up at a football rally? It was something like that.

"But Alex wasn't caught up in the excitement. He was quiet, restrained. Serenely self-confident, I'd say. He took me aside and told me that he was determined to volunteer to go to Russia, if such a thing were still possible. He had the cultural background, he said; spoke the language, looked Russian. It all fit.

"That's what he thought and, as it turned out, that's what our superiors thought. But they made sure he was being led by God, not following some romantic vision. His most severe test was the waiting. He had to go through the early years of training just like the rest of us. We took our vows at the end of the novitiate and spent two years in the juniorate working for our college degrees and three more years studying philosophy and completing the requirements for our degrees.

"Only then was Alex allowed to go to Rome to begin his special studies, about the time the rest of us went off to the high schools. While I was teaching you Latin at Ignatius, Herb, Alex was studying at the *Russicum*, the Jesuits' Russian College in Rome.

"From his letters, it seemed he was getting regular seminary training at the *Russicum,* but he must have been learning how to live and work underground. That's my guess. He never said anything that smacked of the clandestine. He sent me one final letter in 1939, after he'd been ordained. You have it there in the file. It would be his last letter, he said, 'for a long while. Don't try to reply until I send you my new address. It might cause embarrassment here in Rome or elsewhere.' I found that alarming, Herb.

"I never really believed that Alex would actually be sent into the Soviet Union. It didn't seem possible that anyone could get out of Russia in those days, much less sneak in. But I inferred from his letter that he was about to try.

"Not too long after I received Alex's letter, Hitler invaded Poland from the West, Stalin moved in from the East, and then World War II broke out in earnest.

"I didn't expect to hear from Alex during all that chaos, and I didn't. I thought, certainly, I would hear from him after the war ended. But there wasn't a single word from him or about him. Just silence. The years rolled on. I became convinced that he was dead. But I was wrong, thank God.

"A couple of weeks ago, a man from Iowa brought me a letter and two photographs he'd smuggled out of western Siberia. Here, let me show you. The cellophane envelopes are my secretary's idea. Brother Krause thought there might be some fingerprints you could check."

"Were there any fingerprints in your old files?"

"Alex's fingerprints? No. Brother Krause wondered about that, too. He looked but didn't find anything. We never went in for that sort of thing. I don't recall ever being fingerprinted myself, as a matter of fact. Is that a problem?"

"Well, it would have made life easier. So tell me what this man from Iowa had to say."

Father Beck pulled another file from his briefcase. "Here's a copy of Brother Krause's memorandum. He took notes during our meeting and his summary is quite accurate. Verbatim, as far as I can see. He has a remarkable memory."

"I'll look at it later," said Coogan. "First, I want to hear it from you."

Herb Coogan sat back and listened. From time to time, he jotted a note. When Father Beck finished telling him about Harold Hoffmann's visit, he asked: "Do you believe Hoffmann was telling you the truth?"

"The man was badly shaken, Herb, but I think he was trying hard to tell us everything that happened to him. I believe his story."

"How about this Brother Krause? What did he think of Hoffmann and his story?'

"He agrees that Hoffmann had a frightening experience. He thinks his story was, well, 'credible' is the word he used. He was a police detective before becoming a Jesuit."

Coogan smiled. "Once a cop, always a cop," he said. "Now, how about these pictures? You're sure this man is your Father What's-his-name?"

"Samozvanyetz," said Father Beck. "Yes, I'm sure."

"It's been a long time, Father. It's been about 30 years since you've seen him."

"Yes, I know. But look at the eyes, the set of the jaw, the way he stands. The years have taken their toll, but it's Alex. You don't forget someone like Alex Samozvanyetz."

Coogan studied the man in the photographs.

"No," he said, "he doesn't look like the kind of guy you'd easily forget."

Herb turned and stared at J. Edgar Hoover's portrait, drummed his fingers on his desk, then swiveled around to face Father Beck.

"Okay, Father," said Agent-in-Charge Herbert J. Coogan. "Let me see what I can do."

HERB COOGAN'S SECRETARY WAS standing by her desk with her steno pad in her hand when he returned from seeing Father Beck to the elevator.

"Do you want your messages now?" she asked.

"Give me about five minutes."

He sat down at his desk and tried to concentrate, but he couldn't help thinking about Father Beck's remark that the FBI men in the general office looked like accountants. True enough, but those with degrees in Accounting were federal investigators and law enforcement officers now, not just CPAs. There was more to them than met the eye. And the same could be said about the Jesuits he had known.

They all looked like ordinary parish priests: same black suits, same Roman collars, same black cassocks. No special insignia, no special habit, nothing to remind anyone of the order's blood-soaked history: Edmund Campion, drawn and quartered in Elizabethan England; Isaac Jogues and his band of missionaries tortured and killed by the Iroquois; Father Pro hunted down and killed by a firing squad in revolutionary Mexico. And this was the crowd his son Charley was about to get mixed up with.

Herb picked up the photographs Father Beck left with him. He stared hard at the priest in Russia. Herb wondered if Father Campion, Father Jogues and Father Samozvanyetz had all joined the Jesuits because their mothers thought it was a swell idea.

Herb called out to his secretary.

"Send Dan Webster in, will you? I've got some things for him to do."

THE AIRPLANE CARRYING FATHER Beck back to Chicago that afternoon was following the sun and its light shimmered off the wing on his side of the cabin. He lowered the plastic window shade and began to read his Office. The First Lesson was from the First Book of Machabees. Mathathias, the father of Judas Machabeus, was dying and saying to his sons, in Latin:

> "Now have pride and violence grown strong. Now is
> the time for destruction, wrath and indignation. Now
> therefore, my sons, be zealous for the Law and give your
> lives for the covenant of your fathers."

Father Beck sighed. It was hard going, like trying to listen to a radio station that kept fading in and out.

> *"Abraham, nonne in tentationem ventus est fidelis . . ."*

He reread the passage, letting it flow into English.

> "Was not Abraham found faithful in temptation, and it
> was credited to him as justice?"

Father Beck closed his Breviary and lifted the window shade. Enough of that, he thought. He would read his Office later, in privacy and on the ground, not hurtling over the clouds ten thousand feet above the earth.

He often felt out of place in the Old Testament. He

was much more at home on the banks of the Jordan or the shore of the Sea of Galilee. But he was on rocky, unfamiliar ground in much of the Old Testament. He appreciated the poetry and ethics of the ancient scriptures, but he never knew what to make of all the doom and gloom, all the guilt and remorse and despair.

"Now is the time of destruction, wrath and indignation," a dying man was telling his sons today. How grim and how typical of that landscape. He simply did not comprehend the emotional world of the Old Testament. He was a young man when he gave himself to the service of God. And God had rewarded him with years of mostly sunny days.

"Was not Abraham found faithful in temptation?"

What did God's testing of Abraham have to do with John Beck? God had never spoken to him directly. Nor had he a son to offer in sacrifice. He had no idea how he would have handled that life and death decision that was forced upon poor old Abraham. So what lesson was there for him to learn?

As far as he could tell, he had never been tempted to commit a serious sin. But so what? That had to be the case with most people in religious orders and he was indeed grateful that his Jesuit life had delivered him from temptation. But today's reading made him uncomfortable.

Just about everybody in the Bible had been tempted, it seemed. The Scriptures were full of stories of temptation. Abraham, Moses, Simon Peter. Even Christ had been tempted by Satan himself. Why not John Beck?

Looking out across the sunlit clouds, he couldn't recall one completely dark day. There were days when he was concerned about the difficulties experienced by others, even saddened by their trials. He could commiserate. He could comfort. But he had his faith and nothing ever really troubled him except this vague concern about never having been troubled.

"Please fasten your seat belt, Father."

The stewardess was speaking to him with a look of concern.

Had it been so difficult to gain his attention?

Father Beck glanced down at his lap, and then smiled at her.

"It seems I've had it fastened all the way from Cleveland," he said. "But thanks for the reminder."

THE NEXT MORNING, AGENT Daniel Webster, who had done a quick background investigation of the Samozvanyetz family, strolled into Herb Coogan's office with a show of nonchalance.

"Good," said Herb. "You found something?"

"Only a murder," said Webster. "Five years ago. Mrs. Charles Vogel, born Natalie Samozvanyetz. Shot and killed when her house was burglarized. A widow. No children. Her husband had been a professor at Penn State. Died of heart failure ten years after he'd retired. The Vogels lived in Bellefonte, a small town near the university. I talked to the police chief there."

Herb motioned the agent toward a chair. Webster sat down, crossed his legs and consulted his notes.

"Mrs. Vogel, an elderly woman living alone, failed to keep a doctor's appointment. The doctor's nurse called. Mrs. Vogel didn't answer her phone. The nurse called a few more times. Got no response. Finally asked the police to look and see if she was okay. They do that sort of thing in Bellefonte. Officers Pendleton and Moore took the call. No one answered the doorbell. They entered through the side door, which was unlocked. That didn't strike the chief as unusual. I mean, that the door was unlocked or that the officers just went inside. It's a small town and everybody knows everybody, the chief says. Anyway, officers found Mrs. Vogel's body in her bedroom. The coroner estimated she'd been dead for at least two days prior. Killed by a single shot to the head. Slug was recovered. Not the murder weapon. The house burglarized. No stolen property has ever turned up. Case still open. No active leads or suspects.

"I asked about relatives," said Webster, putting his yellow pad aside. "Mrs. Vogel's husband had been dead for several years. The police found some family documents that indicated that Mrs. Vogel's mother and father were dead. Ditto Professor Vogel's parents. He had no brothers or sisters living. Mrs. Vogel had a sister who was a Poor Clare nun in Omaha, Nebraska. She died in 1954. Natural causes."

"What else would a cloistered nun die of?" said Herb.

"Yeah, what else? But I checked anyhow." Webster smiled and went on. "The police learned that Mrs. Vogel had one brother, one Alex Samozvanyetz, who left home to study for the priesthood. They made inquiries, found out he was a Jesuit, so they notified the Jesuit office in Chicago."

"Father Beck didn't mention any murder. He just said the priest's sister died a few years ago."

"Maybe he doesn't know she was murdered," said Webster. He checked his notes. "Detective Paul Mooney made the call. His report said he gave the information to an office worker, one Henrietta Leary. Left his name and phone number. But nobody ever called back for additional information."

"That was it?" Herb asked. "No follow up call to the Jesuits?"

"They didn't see any reason to, I guess," said Webster. "There's not much more. Mrs. Vogel had a small funeral at the local Catholic church. Some neighbors showed up and a couple of elderly professors and their wives from Penn State. And that was that."

"What was missing from the house?"

"Hard to tell. There was nobody to really inventory the place. Radio. Typewriter. That sort of stuff. Nothing heavy like the TV. There was no cash found in the house. No jewelry. The good silverware was gone, according to a neighbor lady. Professor Vogel had a coin collection, she remembered, but there was no sign of it."

"What do the Bellefonte police think?"

"The chief said he thinks someone was passing through

town, saw an opportunity to knock off a house that looked easy, and that Mrs. Vogel got in the way."

"That's what it sounds like," said Herb. "Well, type it up and put it in the file. And make me a copy for Father Beck. He'll have to tell this Father Samozvanyetz about his sister's murder. If we ever get him back, that is."

HERB COOGAN DECIDED TO make a bold move.

He sent an "Eyes Only" report as far up the FBI chain of command as he dared "because of the political sensitivity of this new intelligence."

In his report, he pointed out that Father Samozvanyetz might be an intelligence asset of the highest order. "Because of his many years in Soviet custody," he wrote, "and the many high-level political prisoners with whom he may have associated, this priest may know more than he thinks he knows. Without realizing it, he may have some missing pieces that will allow the Bureau to solve puzzles that have baffled CIA analysts for years." That last line, he thought, would probably do the job.

J. Edgar Hoover would welcome a chance to diminish the influence of his cloak-and-dagger rivals at Langley. The top FBI managers would know that as well. So Herb was confident that the Director himself would soon be reading his last two sentences: "I believe the Bureau, because of our special relationship with this individual's religious superiors, would be most effective in gaining his trust and eliciting information. The Bureau, not the CIA, should conduct this debriefing."

Herb wasn't at all surprised to learn that his report made its way from the FBI to the Justice Department and, almost immediately, to the White House. The U.S. Attorney General and his brother, the President of the United States, were Roman Catholics. Herb assumed that the Kennedy brothers would take a personal interest in his report if it was brought to their attention.

Sure enough, Herb was summoned to Washington and given the assignment he'd been seeking. He was now the agent in charge of the Samozvanyetz case.

BEHIND THE SCENES, THE repatriation of the Jesuit in the USSR was now moving forward secretly, deliberately but slowly. From the beginning of diplomatic negotiations, the Russians seemed willing to allow Father Samozvanyetz to return to the United States. Even so, it took six months to make the arrangements final. His extraction from the Soviet Union was delayed by Khrushchev's escalation of the Berlin crisis and the construction of the Berlin Wall.

The Cold War made it difficult for the two Great Powers to appear to cooperate about anything. But the widely publicized exchange of the Soviet agent Colonel Rudolf Abel for the captured American U-2 pilot Gary Francis Powers would provide enough distraction to allow Father Samozvanyetz to be slipped home without fanfare.

CHAPTER · 7

IT WAS APRIL 26, 1962. The weather in Moscow had turned mild at last.

Wearing civilian clothes, Major Oksana Volkova slid into the back seat of her black sedan. "Hotel Pushkin," she commanded the soldier driving her vehicle. She said no more during the ride across the city.

The big parade was still several days off but construction of the spectator stands in Red Square seemed just about finished. Pilgrims from the provinces stood patiently in the long line around the Kremlin wall waiting to enter Lenin's tomb. Heads turned as her car flashed by. Along the main avenues, workers were covering the walls of buildings with huge portraits and placards emblazoned with party slogans. Tomorrow or the next day, lamp posts and pillars would be draped with red banners. Soon the celebrations would begin. Major Volkova yawned as her sedan sped across a bridge over the river. She had no interest in May Day.

*   *   *

HOTEL PUSHKIN, BUILT BEFORE the Revolution, was on a side street just off a broad boulevard in a residential section of the city, a short ride by taxi to the theaters, museums and office buildings of central Moscow. After the Great Patriotic War, it had been redecorated, renamed and rewired. Muscovites living in the neighborhood whispered that the walls of Hotel Pushkin had ears and the eyes of its staff never blinked.

The hotel did not cater to ordinary tourists. It was reserved for special foreign guests of the state. One such guest had been living at Hotel Pushkin since February, but the matrons at the hall porter's desk on the third floor who presided over the privacy, comfort and morals of the hotel guests, knew nothing about the man in Suite 307 at the end of the hallway. Nothing except his name: Alex Samozvanyetz. Hotel documents listed no other information.

Security men, who used the adjoining Room 305 as a lounge, kept watch on the corridor around the clock. Their job, it seemed, was to keep people away from the man in Suite 307. The guest was under guard, obviously, yet he seemed free to come and go as he pleased. But always with an escort. The women at the desk studied the man every time he passed by. That he was a Russian, not a foreign visitor, they had no doubt. But a Russian from a different age, long before the Revolution. He stirred childhood memories. His was the face on an icon in a village church. Such a face could be seen only in museums now. They could not help but wonder about this Alex Samozvanyetz. What business had a saint in Hotel Pushkin?

Major Oksana Volkova passed through the hotel's revolving front door and stared directly at the pair of stout men who loitered just inside. Observing her straight back and military stride, they quickly looked away.

She surveyed the long lobby with its gray marble columns. In a reception parlor off to the left, a party of Cubans waited with their luggage and their shopping bags. They were going home. Farther down the lobby, just beginning their visit, clusters of Eastern Europeans, Africans and Asians stood separated by race, language and distrust. With each group was an attentive Intourist guide and interpreter.

She marched past guests waiting for the elevators, crossed the lobby and jogged up the marble staircase that rose and split and rose again up through the center of the hotel. On the third floor, eye level with the great crystal chandelier suspended in the stairwell, she paused to catch her breath and then marched toward the hall porter's desk. She flashed her identification in the face of the woman on duty and then strode on toward Suite 307. A young man emerged from the doorway of Room 305, acknowledged her authority and withdrew.

She rapped sharply on the door of Suite 307 and walked inside without waiting for an answer. She hung her hat and topcoat on a wooden peg in the foyer and entered the central room where her man sat alone at the large round dining table, reading. The window was open. White curtains fluttered in the breeze.

"Tomorrow," said Major Volkova.

The man closed his book and stood up. He placed his book atop the upright piano standing against the wall.

"Short notice, Major. After such a long wait."

"I just received word myself. Do you wish to converse in Russian or English?"

"Russian, please. I will have little opportunity to speak the language from now on, I suppose."

"How do you feel?"

"I am somewhat melancholy. I did not think I would feel this way."

He walked to the china cabinet, opened the glass doors and took out a bottle of vodka and two short stemmed pink crystal glasses. "The Prisoner of Chillon regains his freedom with a sigh," he said.

Major Volkova let it pass without comment.

"Let us sit in the parlor," he said, gesturing to the door of an adjoining room. "It is more comfortable."

"Everything came together all at once," Major Volkova said brusquely. She sat down in an upholstered armchair and arranged her skirt. "All the arrangements have been made. Your plane leaves for Paris tomorrow morning. You will leave the hotel by six."

He sat down on the sofa and placed the bottle and the two glasses on the low table in front of him. "So," he said as he poured, "tomorrow is the day. I wonder if I shall ever see Russia again."

He handed her a glass of vodka. "To Mother Russia, then?"

Major Volkova drained her glass and placed it on the table.

"You will leave everything here and take nothing with you."

"I know. All my papers are there on the desk," he said. "And most of the money you gave me, as well. I did not spend much."

"It is important that you take nothing with you, you understand. No documents, no souvenirs."

"Yes," he said. "I understand. Just the clothes on my back. A louse on a leash in one pocket, a flea on a chain in the other."

"Please spare me your *zek* talk. I have expressed sufficient regrets for your ordeal, I believe."

"You have, of course. There are no hard feelings, Major."

"The prisoner-priest is most forgiving."

"It is the function of priests to forgive."

She accepted a second glass but took only a sip.

"We have both survived, you must admit."

"Yes, we have," he said. "It has been difficult, but we have both survived."

"And your Anya has survived as well. We must never forget Anya."

Major Volkova was smiling but her eyes were cold.

"Will I see Anya before I leave?"

"I am afraid not."

"I had hoped to say farewell."

"She is away on an assignment. I could not get her back

to Moscow in time. As I said, everything fell into place more quickly than I expected."

"If I write her a note, will you give it to her?"

"Of course. But be careful what you say. She has no idea who you really are."

He shrugged. "It is probably better that she is not here."

"I think so."

Major Volkova looked toward the open window. "I need not remind you that Anya will remain under my personal protection."

She took another sip of vodka and waited for that to register.

"Let us now talk about Alex Samozvanyetz and his future," she said. "Going home may be difficult for you at first. So many years have passed, but it is always better to deal with the present and the future. The past is mostly illusion. Memory seldom provides an accurate record. It retains perceptions and impressions of how things seemed to be at the time. Some things vanish from the memory completely. Concern yourself with the present and the future. Lapses of memory should cause you no problems."

"Yes," he said. "A new situation can be dealt with. But it is frightening, nevertheless, to consider how many things must have changed over the years."

"They have changed for everybody. You will adapt to changes as you become aware of them. Actually," she said as she stood up, "there is not much past for you to go home to, I suspect. But you will learn the fate of friends and family when you get there."

She walked to the windows, parted the curtains and looked down onto the street. Her sedan was parked beyond the row of taxicabs, as she had ordered.

"I must leave now," she said. "I will not be here in the morning to see you off."

She turned and directed his eyes to the light fixture in the ceiling. She cupped her ear and he nodded.

"I thank you for stopping by today, Major. Perhaps you would allow me to escort you to your automobile?"

"That would be most courteous."

They did not speak again until they were outside the hotel, walking along the sidewalk toward her car.

"There is something you should know before you leave," she said. "I do not know exactly when, but soon, the Party will denounce Stalin officially and publicly. He will be blamed for everything that has ever gone wrong. How far this public repudiation will go, I have no idea. But the KGB has been spreading rumors of this in the West for some time now. People in the United States already know more about this than people here, I am sure. So when American intelligence officers interrogate you, as they certainly will, do not worry about telling them what you know about Lubianka and the camps. What you say will harm nobody here. Not me and not Anya."

"Thank you for telling me that. It makes me less apprehensive."

"I thought it would. Well, Father Alex Samozvanyetz, let me wish you a safe journey. Do not worry about the future," she said with her cold smile. "I will never be far away."

HE RETURNED TO HIS suite and read until his eyes grew tired. He set his book aside and sat quietly in his parlor for a while. Morning would come all too quickly, so he decided to have supper in his rooms and go to bed early. But, before that, he would take one last walk.

He knocked on the door of the room next to his suite. "I thought I would stroll down to the river," he said. The youngest of the security men stood up. "I would welcome the exercise," said the young man.

THE SUN WAS LEAVING the sky and taking the springtime warmth with it, but he was wearing a heavy sweater under his jacket. He leaned on the railing of the embankment and gazed across the river. The city of Moscow murmured in the distance.

He watched a boat chugging upstream. The reflections of the lights on the bridges shimmered like diamonds in the small craft's wake. Across the water he could see the flood-lit domes of the churches and the red stars glowing atop the spires of government buildings.

He watched as Day surrendered to Night. And then there was no color in the sky, only the white and red lights provided by Man and the State. They obscured the lights from God's stars, so far away. He turned and put Moscow behind him.

The young man walked with him in silence through the darkness back toward the hotel.

The glow of a street lamp spilled through the branches of a leafless tree down onto the pavement. He walked through puddles of light, in Limbo so it seemed to him, passing through a long tunnel that ran from the past to a future somewhere up ahead in the dark. His silent companion kept step, but he was alone in the night.

The fear was familiar. He had felt it often enough though the years. But he had managed to stay alive through everything. One had to stay alive, but at what cost? In surviving, how much of his true self had he lost? *Who am I really?* he wondered. *After all this, who am I now? At this exact moment?*

It was not until he left the darkness of the suburban streets and returned to his lighted rooms that he felt any peace at all. Later, after the maid had cleared away his half eaten supper, he settled into bed.

Before falling to sleep, he was able to say to himself: "I am Alex Samozvanyetz. I am a Jesuit priest and a citizen of the United States. Tomorrow morning, I am going home."

THE SECURITY MEN RAPPED on his door precisely at six o'clock. He had been up since five. He had bathed and shaved and toyed with the breakfast laid out on the dining room table. The eggs were cold, but the bread and lukewarm tea settled his stomach. He felt less anxious having eaten something.

He packed his shaving kit, a clean shirt and two sets of clean underwear into his small black satchel, and then he had nothing else to do but sit and wait for the knock at the door. It came at last and the three security men took him down the elevator, through the lobby and out the front door to a brown sedan parked in front of the hotel.

He sat in the back seat. The young security man sat beside him; the other two sat in front. His escorts were professional men, not given to small talk. He understood that, but the silence deepened his sense of isolation. From the back seat of the car on the way to the airport, he watched sadly as a grove of white birch trees sailed past his window.

Inside the terminal, while other passengers waited in long lines to have their tickets and passports and luggage examined by uniformed officials, he and his escorts stood apart waiting for the boarding announcement, not looking at each other, shuffling around the small black satchel resting on the floor. Was he an old uncle being seen off on a journey by his dutiful nephews? So it might seem.

It was finally time to leave. The young man who had walked with him to the river the night before held his hand in a strong grip. "I have enjoyed our walks together," he said, "and I wish you a safe journey." The others shook his hand solemnly and muttered formal farewells. They stood there watching him until he boarded the airplane. And they would wait until the plane took off, he knew.

From the air, as the aircraft rose up along its curving path of departure, he could make out factories, apartment buildings and smaller dwellings, but not the river or the city itself. He could not take the sight of the Kremlin with him, only the white birch trees along the road. Haze soon covered the land below; he could see no ground at all.

The four engines of the Aeroflot plane were growling in English: "Where-are-you? Where-are-you? Where-are-you?"

Yes, he thought, where am I? Lost, he feared. Somewhere in the past he had lost himself: in his training for a life of deception, in the interrogation room, in the prison cell or in the labor camp, somewhere his true self had been buried deep underground.

The airplane continued to climb through the overcast. Gradually, the light outside became brighter, the clouds less dense. Then, suddenly, he was thrust into the brilliance of the cloudless atmosphere. He raised his hand to cut off the sunlight and turned away from the window. The light was so intense, he could not see. He closed his eyes and, finally, fell asleep.

THE AEROFLOT AIRPLANE LANDED near Paris in a light rain. He had only one glimpse of the city through a break in the clouds. No matter. He sat with his black satchel in his lap waiting, according to instructions, for the other passengers to disembark. He watched the flight crew leave. They did not even glance in his direction.

A man entered the door at the front of the cabin. He

shook the rain off his hat as he walked deliberately down the aisle. He opened the satchel and looked through its contents.

"You have left everything else in Moscow? Empty your pockets, just to be sure." Satisfied, the man led him down the aisle and out the door.

The air was warm and the rain barely a drizzle. Parked alongside the airplane were two vehicles: an unmarked black sedan and a light gray van with a yellow flasher on its roof. Standing at the bottom of the stairs were two groups of men in hats and raincoats. They waited for him to descend. Once on solid ground, his Russian escort looked at his American counterpart.

"This is your man," he said in English.

"Thank you very much, Boris," said the leader of the Americans. "You can give me his bag, if you will. We'll handle it from here. Perhaps I'll see you in Geneva this summer? At the conference?"

"Perhaps," said the Russian. "I do not know if I will be there."

"Well, if not there, someplace else, I'm sure. Always nice doing business with you, Boris."

The American led him to the van.

"In you go, if you please," he said quietly. "Let's get the hell out of here."

Once inside, with the doors closed and the van moving, the man turned and said, "Welcome back, Father Samozvanyetz. We think it's best to press on to New York, if you're up to it. We'll get some rest in New York, then fly on to Cincinnati and drive you to the Jesuit Novitiate in Milford, Ohio. We've been told it's very quiet. Very private."

"Unless things have changed, it is extremely quiet. I wonder if I will know anybody there after all these years."

"I think you will. Father John Beck is there now. He's the one who received your letter."

"I can't believe it! John Beck, my old friend, alive and well, waiting for me. I never expected anything so . . ." He searched for a word and chose "miraculous."

He spent most of the flight across the Atlantic preparing for Mass, reciting the prayers under his breath. "*Introibo ad altare Dei . . .*"

Soon, he thought, he would be standing at the foot of a real altar, clad in proper vestments, holding a shrouded chalice, acolytes by his side, candles flickering. But now, in the darkened cabin, he repeated the Latin prayers over and over again in his mind. By the time the sun overtook the airplane and tinged the clouds with gold and rose, he had recited the Ordinary of the Mass, from Introit to Last Gospel, at least half a dozen times.

THE LAST LEG OF the journey was the shortest, from New York to Cincinnati where there was a changing of the guard. His new protectors were agents of the Federal Bureau of Investigation and they were led by a man named Coogan who, he was quick to say, had studied under Father John Beck in high school.

"He's really looking forward to seeing you, Father," Coogan said as they walked out of the terminal. His face was quite open and he looked—what was the expression? Pleased as punch?

The Cincinnati airport was south of the city on the Kentucky side of the Ohio River, so Coogan told him as he helped him into the passenger seat of the blue four-door sedan. The car soon crossed a bridge over the Ohio River near a point on the map where a tributary, the Little Miami River, he remembered, begins to meander in a north easterly direction through the rolling countryside.

Through the open windows, mild spring air filled the car with the moist scent of freshly plowed earth. The hills were soft and green in the late afternoon sunlight. Coogan took him at moderate speed along a tree lined road. He saw wild flowers in bloom, those yellow flowers called daffodils and those tall purple flowers whose name he could not recall immediately. Flags. Yes, flags. Which he saw through the iris of his eye? No, not the iris. The lens. But the flags were also irises.

He was driven past small farms whose tidy white houses were enclosed by white wooden fences. Down along the riverside, when the stream could be seen through the trees, he glimpsed dark tar-papered fishing lodges, small shacks really, built on top of wooden poles.

Then came the houses of the people in the quiet town of Milford, then the rattling iron bridge that spanned the Little Miami, some more tree shaded residences and, finally, at the end of a side street, the two stone cairns marking the entrance to the drive that led up the low hill to the Novitiate.

He filled his chest with air as the sedan climbed slowly up the narrow roadway through shafts of light that slanted down through breaks in the pine trees. Beyond the tall bare trunks he could see part of the ivy covered brick building.

And then he saw the novices!

Cassocks swirling, four abreast, they were walking down the roadway through the pines. Coogan stopped the car to let them march past, almost a hundred of them, more or less in step, heads bowed, eyes downcast, rosary beads held in clasped hands. Not one of them even glanced at the car. He heard the *Dux* leading the chant:

"*Ave Maria, gratia plena, Dominus tecum. Benedicta tu in mulieribus et benedictus fructus ventris tui, Jesus.*" The marching novices chanted their response: "*Sancta Maria, Mater Dei, ora pro nobis peccatoribus, nunc et in hora mortis nostrae. Amen.*"

The young men wheeled about, cassocks opening to reveal brown trousers and shoes some had brought from home.

Coogan, keeping a respectful distance, followed the chanting novices up the roadway for a hundred yards or so, then turned left onto the drive that led to the main building. Beyond the Novitiate, rising above the hedges that marked the cloister limits, was the small green hill with its low white markers. Beyond the cemetery stretched the playing fields and, off to one side, the two concrete hand-ball courts.

The car came to a halt in front of the wide stone stair-way that led up to the main entrance. His journey was over.

He climbed out of the passenger seat and looked at the large white statue of the Sacred Heart that still faced the Novitiate. He stood for a moment, looking up at the statue. The figure of Christ stood humbly, heart exposed, arms opened in acceptance. He remembered another such figure, a man who had suddenly appeared before him many years before. He turned away from the pain. Looking up toward the front doors of the building, he saw the priest standing at the top of the grey stone staircase dressed in black, not robes of white like the statue, but welcoming him with open arms.

It was John Beck. There could be no doubt.

He hurried up the stone stairs and cried: "I am home, John!"

He fell to his knees. "Please, John, may I have your blessing?"

He waited, eyes closed, while the Sign of the Cross was made above his head and heard John Beck intone: "*Pax et benedictio Dei omnipotentis, Patris et Filii, et Spiritus Sancti, descendat super te et maneat semper.*"

He felt the priest's hands on his head and he responded: "*Amen.*"

John Beck grasped him by the shoulders and raised him up. "Let me have a look at you, Alex."

He saw the tears in John Beck's eyes.

"John, my dear friend! I thought I'd never see you again!"

"I never stopped praying for you, Alex."

"And, here I am! Home at last, John!" He pulled a handkerchief from his pocket and blew his nose. "Tell me, John," he said. "Will there be pie for supper?"

John Beck stared at him for a moment. Then, remembering the banter of their days as novices, exploded with laughter.

"You bet there'll be pie for supper, Alex. And maybe ice cream, too."

HE WAITED WHILE JOHN Beck opened the front door of the novitiate, but he did not enter immediately.

Behind him, through the spring air scented with pine and lilac, he heard the voices of the novices, strong in unison, chanting the rosary like some tragic chorus. He turned and looked back over the grounds, over the head of the FBI agent Coogan who was carrying his black satchel up the stairs.

From here, he could see everything, and everything was in its proper place. The cemetery was up the knoll off to the right, the statue of the Sacred Heart directly ahead. On the roadway behind the statue, the marching novices were now chanting the Litany, the chorused responses rhythmic and energetic. "*Ora pro nobis, ora pro nobis, ora pro nobis.*"

He took a deep breath. The trees were taller, the hedges higher. Otherwise, everything seemed unchanged by time. He turned and walked confidently into the Novitiate.

Everything was exactly as Father Alex Samozvanyetz had remembered it.

CHAPTER · 8

BROTHER NILS HEGSTAD, THE tall balding man who ran the novitiate infirmary, always had trouble remembering names. He served as a medical corpsman in the Pacific during World War II and sometimes, in the night, wounded marines would call out to him. In his dreams, he was always "Corpsman" or "Medic." They were always "Buddy" or "Sarge" or "Sir." He never recalled their given names; he recognized them by their wounds. When he awoke, he remembered them in his prayers.

At Milford, there was no need to call anybody by name. Brother Hegstad liked that. All novices were "Carissime" and all juniors were "Mister." Priests were "Father," except for "Father Rector," the superior of the community, and "Father Minister," who was a combination treasurer and supply sergeant. The "Misters" who pursued their college studies in the other wing of the H-shaped building, had a Dean in charge of them. But he was just "Father" like the rest of the priests. Ditto the Master of Novices.

Brother Hegstad's infirmary, tucked away on the third floor of the novice's wing, was even more orderly and quiet than the novitiate itself. He had nothing more ghastly to deal with now than minor athletic injuries, common colds and a few cases of homesickness, which he treated with bed, rest, cinnamon toast, Jell-O and ice cream. At the moment, he had only one patient in his infirmary, the visiting Father who had slept twelve hours straight when he arrived.

"Our visitor needs his rest," Father Rector had told the community assembled in the main chapel. "Please respect his privacy with charity and patience. Don't pry. Your curiosity will be satisfied eventually, but not right now."

Brother Hegstad's patient had arrived fairly worn out from his long journey, but he wasn't sick and required no special attention. He stayed in his room, took his meals in the infirmary and said Mass every morning in the small chapel down the hall, once the novices had cleared out of their dormitory rooms. Brother Hegstad served as his acolyte. "Father" said Mass real slow. Brother Hegstad liked that.

A doctor from out of town—Washington, he said—came to give Father a thorough physical examination and Brother Hegstad assisted him. "Doctor" had some suggestions about rest and diet with which Brother Hegstad agreed. "He's in pretty good shape, considering his age, but make sure he takes it easy for a while."

The doctor had more to say to Herb Coogan and Father Beck.

"It's obvious that he's been through quite an ordeal. Everything you'd expect for a prison camp survivor. Exposure to the elements. Poor diet bordering on malnutrition. He should see a dentist one of these days, but there's nothing urgent. The man has one hell of a constitution. Heart and lungs sound. Muscle tone good. Nothing seriously wrong with him that I can see. I'll call you with the lab results when I get back to Washington, but I don't anticipate any surprises. How tough are you going to be on him?"

"Not tough at all," said Coogan. "A very informal debriefing. Just Father Beck and me, a Jesuit lay brother to record the minutes, maybe a couple of observers from D.C."

"Well, if you're not going to make a big deal out of it," said the doctor, "you can start whenever you want. But don't try to get it all done in one day."

When "Doctor" left for Washington, Brother Hegstad noted that he took with him the black satchel and all the clothing and toilet articles "Father" had brought out of Russia. "Doctor" didn't bother to say why.

IT WAS FATHER BECK'S idea to use the retreat house at the far end of the novitiate's property for the debriefing session. Laymen from Cincinnati stayed in the two-story wooden structure when they came to Milford for weekend spiritual exercises. The building had its own kitchen and dining room, and a conference room where the Jesuit retreat masters prepared the laymen for their private meditations. The bedrooms were on the second floor.

"You and your men won't even be noticed," Father

Beck told Herb Coogan when he showed him through the building. "Laymen walking around this section of the grounds are a familiar sight here. So what do you think? Will this place suit you?"

"It sure will," said Coogan. "Takes me back to my army days. Looks like my old barracks died and went to Heaven."

"Well, maybe Purgatory, Herb. It's been renovated, but it's not the Ritz."

"We're not looking for luxury, Father."

"Just as well, because you won't find it. But what are you looking for?"

"I honestly don't know," said Coogan. "We're always looking for anything new about the Soviet Union, of course. But Father Samozvanyetz is an unusual case. That's why we're keeping quiet about him. If we find out anything that might affect relations with the Soviet Union, President Kennedy wants to know about it before he reads it in the papers. He's made that very clear. He was happy he could get your guy repatriated, but he doesn't want it to backfire on him politically. So he wants to have all the right answers before reporters and congressmen start asking questions."

"I'm sure that's the best way to proceed," said Father Beck. "For the government and the Society, too. Is that why I'm participating in this exercise?"

"You're involved because I insisted you be involved, Father. Part of a debriefing is determining the credibility of the person providing the information. I'm counting on you to pick up on things I may miss."

"Like what, Herb?"

"I have no idea. Just don't react if you hear something that bothers you, but be sure to tell me about it later, when we're alone."

FATHER SAMOZVANYETZ SEEMED RESTED and in a good mood when Father Beck brought him to the retreat house for the first day of debriefing. He shook hands with Brother Al Krause who would be representing the Chicago Province and recording the minutes; Agent Coogan, whom he knew, and Professor Mitchell Sloane, who would be representing the U.S. Attorney General.

"And where is the CIA?" asked Father Samozvanyetz, pretending to survey the conference room. "Under the table, perhaps?"

"No CIA," said Herb Coogan. "This is a very private affair, Father. Only a very few of us know that you're even here."

"That's fine with me," said Father Samozvanyetz.

He walked to the sideboard and poured himself a mug of coffee.

"My, doesn't this place bring back memories! This is where Father Beck and I lived while the main building was being constructed. We were among the Missouri Province novices who came here by train from Florissant. That was back in 1927. I hope you gentlemen find it more comfortable than we did back then. It was pretty cold and drafty in the winter."

He took his seat at the head of the table. "So, let us begin," said Father Samozvanyetz. "What do you want to know?"

"Father has back grounded us on the Russian Mission," said Sloane. "We might want some specific information about your training in Rome, but we can come back to that later if we feel we need to. Let's start with how you got into the Soviet Union in the first place."

"Yes, of course," said Father Samozvanyetz. "Well, it wasn't all that difficult, as it turned out. Not as difficult as I'd anticipated, certainly. It was simply a matter of not calling attention to myself, moving forward without doing anything unusual at any given place or time.

"For example, when I left the Jesuit house in Rome to begin my journey, I was just another priest taking a leisurely stroll, but I was really walking to the train station with a ticket in my pocket. Once there, I went to the baggage check room and claimed a suitcase, which had been left for me the day before. Then I boarded the train to Vienna. I must have been excited, but I can't recall my exact feelings. It was very hot and uncomfortable, I remember, until the train began moving. Nobody asked me any questions. A priest on a train. Who cared?

"There was confusion all about and much talk of war. I remember the speculation in Rome among the people, the conferences with my superiors at the Russicum, the decision that I should prepare to leave for Poland. Apparently the Vatican had learned of something long before the general public for there was nothing in the newspapers when I left to indicate any change in the general situation. But my superiors told me the wind was right, the hour had come and it was time to go. So I walked to the station and took the train to Vienna.

"It was a time of confusion, as I said, but everyone was trying to behave in a calm, civilized manner. It was important to behave as if everything was normal and would continue to be so. Did people believe that correct behavior could forestall inevitable disaster? That calm could prevent the storm? Perhaps they did. Perhaps that's why I had no difficulty taking the train to Vienna and then taking another train to Warsaw. I had no trouble getting a seat. Not many people were headed in that direction.

"When I arrived at the Vienna train station, I saw a great many German soldiers. They were returning from leave to rejoin their units, I supposed. It was common knowledge that the Germans were massing troops along the Polish border. I was afraid I might have some problems getting through customs and passport control. But, again, everything went smoothly. I approached an official with a Nazi swastika armband. I presented myself as an American Jesuit on his way to one of our houses of study in Poland. He looked at me as if I was mad, but he said nothing. He gave my passport a cursory glance and passed me through the gate.

"It was much different at the train station in Warsaw. The Poles greeted me warmly, as if I'd come to join them in the defense of their country. The customs official didn't even open my suitcase. Instead, he asked me to pray for Poland. I can see him now, the poor man: a brave smile and a gold tooth, right here, in the front of his mouth. I assured him that I would indeed pray for Poland. And I did."

He smiled at Father Beck. "So much for my understanding of prayer, John. I was young and naïve and still quite smug, I'm afraid." He shook his head. Then he brightened suddenly. "Here's something I remember quite well. It changed everything. But let me explain something first.

"I'd been following my instructions to make my way to the Jesuit theolgate at Lvov where I'd be told how to proceed into Russia. I suppose there was something like an underground railroad, but my superiors never gave me any specific information about that. No matter. I never reached Lvov.

"What happened was this. I was walking through the Warsaw train station, following my orders, looking for the train to Lvov. Music was coming from loudspeakers. They'd been set up to carry the broadcasts of Radio Warsaw. I remember hearing the music as I walked along: something by Chopin. Then the music stopped abruptly. People in the train station fell silent.

"A voice reverberated through the terminal. The German foreign minister—von Ribbentrop, was that his name? He was flying to Moscow to sign an agreement with the Soviet Union. The radio announcer called it a non-aggression pact.

"The Poles in the station stood frozen in their tracks. So did I. We all knew what the news meant. Hitler had secured Stalin's promise of neutrality. German armies could march into Poland without fear of Soviet opposition or interference. An invasion of Poland was not only possible now, it could happen at any moment. Suddenly there was turmoil. If Radio Warsaw resumed playing music, I couldn't hear it over the clamor of voices.

"Now what was I to do? My orders were to go to Russia. That was the purpose of all my training. There was no point in going on to Lvov just to become a captive of the Germans. I had to improvise, to head to the East on my own and take my chances. I left the train station with my suitcase and walked into the city.

"I found a quiet park and sat there on a bench until dusk, keeping my eye on a nearby church, not too big, not too small, until I saw the sexton close the front doors, locking up for the night. I hoped he was getting ready to go home to his supper. I hurried across the park to the church and found the sacristy door on the side of the church and knocked. The door opened almost immediately. The sexton looked exasperated, but he relaxed when he saw I was a priest.

"I told him, in Polish, that I had a long wait between trains and wanted a quiet place to read my Office. Perhaps I could sit in his church? But I could see he was leaving. Never mind, I told him; I'll try to find someplace else.

"But the sexton said, 'No, no, no, Father,' and waved

me inside. He showed me how to switch off the lights and how to lock the sacristy door when I left. He asked me to remember him in my prayers and went home to his family. As soon as he left, I locked the door after him and went underground. Quite literally.

"I lit a candle and crept into the darkened church where I found a stairway that led down to a crypt below the main altar. Candle in one hand, suitcase in the other, I crept down the stone steps to a vaulted chamber with deceased priests and parishioners interred in its walls. Off to one side stood a sarcophagus. I hoisted my suitcase onto its lid and unpacked my new identity.

"I laid out a working man's traveling wardrobe: hat, coat, sweater, trousers, a pair of worn but sturdy boots, extra socks and underwear, a few toilet articles, and a haversack to sling over my shoulder. The suitcase had a false bottom. The hidden compartment contained two old leather wallets, which held some money and forged identity papers—one wallet for Poland, one for the Soviet Union. I hid the Russian one in the lining of my haversack.

"I stripped naked and turned out the pockets of the clothes I'd been wearing to make sure they held nothing to identify the Jesuit priest from Rome. Then I packed everything I had worn on my trip into the suitcase and got dressed in the clothes I'd worn while doing manual labor at the Russicum. The clothes were familiar and comfortable. I slipped the Polish money and documents into my coat pocket and became a Pole, at least for the time being.

"I slid the suitcase into the dead space behind the sarcophagus and the wall of the crypt and pushed it as far as it would go. Anything that marked me as a priest was out of sight, entombed in the crypt.

"Standing there in the gloom and dampness, the candlelight and the cobwebs, I felt very clever indeed. I smiled a conspirator's smile. Very much the daring secret agent, I slipped back up the stairs. The church was still empty and I swaggered to the sacristy. Before blowing out my candle, I took one last look around. There were vestments laid out for the first Mass of the morning. The chasuble was red as blood. But I had no intention of becoming a martyr myself.

"Such arrogance! I thought I was not going to get caught because God had such important work for me to do. At least I had enough sense to kneel down and pray. Before I slipped out into the night, I made sure the sacristy door was locked tight behind me.

"In Rome I'd been told of a safe place to stay in Warsaw, a small working man's hotel that I found without difficulty. My Polish was good enough to get me a meal and a room for the night. I ate at a common table with some men who were exchanging rumors. Some had a lot to say. Others just listened. I chewed my food and listened with an occasional nod of agreement. I was a dullard with nothing of interest to contribute. Nobody asked me any questions.

"The talk was of war. The alliance between the Russians and the Germans, all agreed, meant Hitler was free to attack. But did it mean that the Soviet Union would also attack Poland? Some said yes and some said no. No one had any facts. The futile discussion was still going on when I wiped my chin, bid everyone a goodnight and went upstairs to bed.

"Before retiring—I'd been given a small room all to myself—I took my straight razor and sliced my American passport into tiny bits. I shredded it all, the cover as well as all the pages. I put the fragments in a paper bag along with my shredded train tickets. I stuffed the bag into my jacket pocket. Next morning, after a sound sleep, I ate breakfast with the other workingmen and set off toward Brest Litovsk. First by bus and then on foot.

"I had no way of knowing what route other Jesuits might have taken to get into the Soviet Union. I'd no idea of how to get past the Russian border guards. My plan, such as it was, was simply to head east as slowly as possible. If war broke out soon, which seemed more and more likely, some opportunity to cross the border undetected would probably present itself. In the confusion, I might even be able to join a crowd of refugees fleeing to the East.

"I avoided the large towns and it was, by and large, a pleasant journey: a stroll through the rolling countryside which was not so much different from our Ohio countryside. There were a lot of small farms with pigs and chickens and geese, and villages clustered around stone churches. Mostly I walked on dirt roads through patches of woodland and along open fields almost ready for harvest. During the first week of my journey, I had the roads to myself except for a passing truck or cart. I got rid of my shredded American identity—a little piece here, a little piece there—as I walked to the East. The skies were blue and almost cloudless. The air was warm and dry. Perfect weather for a hike in the country.

"Out in the countryside, war seemed unlikely and unreal. But there was fearful speculation in every village I passed through and in every home in which I spent the night. I was now a merchant seaman, you see, a sailor on his way home to his own village on the Russian border after many years away at sea. I had a bag full of tall tales to distract the country folks. They were as eager to hear about far-away places as they were generous in their hospitality. So I never lacked for a meal to eat or a place to sleep. I'd spend the night, go to morning Mass in the village church, buy some bread and cheese to eat during the day and be on my way.

"The war, when it did start that first week in September, was something that was happening far, far away to the West. But late one morning, getting on toward noon, I got a clear view of the real war.

"I'd followed a dirt road up a little hill to a grove of trees where I sat in the shade with my back against a tree, ate my bread and cheese and washed it down with a little wine my hosts had pressed upon me. Before me stretched golden fields waiting for the harvesters and green pastures where cattle grazed. Beyond the fields I could see grey village buildings gathered, as if for protection, around a church with a tall, slender spire.

"It was a warm, peaceful day. I was sweaty from the morning's walk, but there was a slight breeze and it was cool under the tree. I was lulled by the humming of the insects and the chirping of the birds. I dozed for a while. For how long, I don't know. But I became conscious of another humming sound, a pulsating drone more insistent than the buzzing insects.

"I was hearing aircraft engines. I was wide awake now, but I wasn't frightened. The sound of aircraft motors harmonized with the other sounds. I looked about the sky, but not with any sense of urgency or anxiety. I was not even frightened when I finally saw the airplanes.

'There were three of them, dark against the cloudless blue sky. They seemed to glide together through the air without obvious purpose and they reminded me of the turkey buzzards I used to see around here in the afternoon, soaring aimlessly through the air on motionless wings.

"I watched the planes much as I used to watch the buzzards, with mild interest but certainly no apprehension. The three airplanes slowly followed a curving line of flight, which took them directly over the village and beyond. Now I could barely hear their engines.

"Then I saw bright flashes on the ground. Quick flashes of sunlight. Clouds of dust and smoke. Then came the sounds of explosions: like an irregular beating on a shrouded bass drum. Thump-whump. Thump-whump-whump. Thump, thump. I couldn't count the number. I sat staring at the thick column of black smoke rising above the village, hanging there, drifting slightly in the blue sky above the green and golden fields.

"It was over in a matter of minutes. The spire of the church was gone. I could see no buildings, just the black smoke rising. I'd been sitting there with my back against the tree, the taste of bread and cheese and wine in my mouth, watching quietly while God knows how many people died before my eyes. I know I tried to pray for those poor souls. But my prayers were mechanical, dry as dust.

"I could not comprehend what I'd seen. The peaceful countryside had been struck by violence and death just a few miles away, but the breeze still whispered through my little grove of trees. Birds sang, insects hummed. Nothing had touched my hill. That was the war I saw, my friends. The rest, I just heard about."

Father Samozvanyetz lowered his head and reached for the glass of water to his right. He held it in his hand, regarding it for a moment before drinking from it.

"The man I see in my memory is young, very young," he said quietly. "I see him now, this brash young priest marching bravely toward the East, his pack slung over his shoulder, his heart full of innocent arrogance. He seems almost a stranger. Father Beck has reminded me that I shouldn't judge him too harshly.

"But I am rambling. I see that you want me to get on with my story, isn't that right? How did this crazy young priest get across the Russian border? Well, I can't take credit for any brilliant maneuver. As it turned out, I did not cross the Russian border. The Russian border crossed me."

Father Beck stood up. "I think it's time for a break," he said. "There are more toilets upstairs, if anybody needs one."

CHAPTER · 9

"SESSION 2," BROTHER KRAUSE wrote in his fresh notebook and began to record what he heard in shorthand.

"It was several days after I witnessed the bombing of the village. Almost a week, I think," said Father Samozvanyetz when the group in the retreat house reassembled.

"I had passed well to the south of Brest-Litovsk which I assumed would be a military target. I didn't want to be captured by the Germans, so I stayed far away from urban areas and kept to the dirt roads that headed east through the countryside.

"I began encountering more and more people heading to the West with household goods piled into carts and wagons. These refugees had not seen any Russian troops, but they were afraid that the Red Army was about to occupy this part of Poland. They had just packed up and headed west, one old man told me, because they feared Stalin more than they feared Hitler. He thought I was crazy to be heading east. He became so excited that he shouted at me and called me a fool before turning away in disgust. I was amused by his outburst, but he did make me more cautious.

"Fear had caused people to abandon their ancestral homes and villages. Any stranger heading upstream against the current toward certain death, as they saw it, would certainly be the subject of speculation among the refugees and I certainly didn't want that. I wanted to become inconspicuous. So, from then on, when I saw people approaching from the east, I sat down by the side of the road and pretended to be resting. I always sat facing west.

"How clever I felt as people passed by with hardly a glance at this straggler they had overtaken on the road. Little did they know that I had just come from where they were going. I was so pleased that they never suspected that I was on my way to where they had been.

"I soon found out how clever I really was. What I next ran into was the Red Army."

Father Samozvanyetz shook his head. "Have you ever seen an army on the move? It's an impressive sight, let me tell you. I became aware of the Red Army before I saw it.

"The ground did not tremble. That wasn't the sensation. Just a murmuring in the air at first, low and deep, slowly increasing in power like some force of nature. I could see only open fields and a few farm buildings here and there, but no people.

"Everything around me had fallen silent. The birds had stopped singing. Even the insects were still. There was just this ominous undertone, this growing presence. Something awesome like a tidal wave or an avalanche was steadily approaching.

"A few yards up the road, off to the left, there was a small patch of woods. I ran there, dropped my haversack and climbed a tree to look out ahead across the rolling countryside.

"Russia was moving towards me! All of it! All of Russia, it seemed. An ocean of men and machines flooded the roads and the fields, an enormous tidal wave that flowed toward me from the eastern horizon and stretched to the north and to the south as far as I could see. Columns of trucks and cannons in advance of a mass of humanity. I couldn't discern individual soldiers or vehicles, just the relentlessly approaching deluge.

"How much time did I have until the Red Army engulfed me? The hill in front of me partially blocked my view. I couldn't see what was moving up the road I was on. I suddenly realized that I was in a terrible spot. What better hiding place for a lookout or a sniper, up there in the branches of a tree? I clambered down as quickly as I could.

"Here I was, the only civilian within miles. A civilian with one too many identities. The plan to transform myself into a Russian had seemed foolproof in Rome. Now it was obviously absurd. What would a Russian be doing in Poland at this time and in this place? Should I try to make the Russian identity papers work? No, that would take a quickly improvised, masterful lie. And if I couldn't carry it off, I would be taken for a spy and shot on the spot.

"Should I continue to be the Polish merchant seaman? The Poles had taken me for a Pole. But how good were the Polish identity papers? No one had examined them as closely as the Russians would.

"Better to have no papers at all. I could claim that I had lost everything when my village was bombed. I was lucky to have escaped with my life. All I cared about now was getting revenge on the Germans. That seemed plausible enough. Would it stand up to intense investigation? I would just have to take my chances. But time was running out. The Red Army was advancing.

"A small creek ran through the woods. I built a small fire on its bank and burned my Polish and Russian money, my forged documents, my spare socks and underwear, even my haversack. I pushed the ashes into the water and watched all of it drift downstream. My razor, my pocketknife, the buckles of my haversack, all the things that wouldn't burn I threw as far as I could into the underbrush.

"Then I ran out of the woods as fast as I could to get back onto the road. Better to meet the Red Army out in the open. The Russian soldiers would see an unarmed civilian who posed no threat.

"Once I reached the road, I stopped running and resumed walking at a slow, steady pace. By the time I saw the first soldiers approaching, I was breathing normally.

"There were three of them coming over the rise. They pointed their rifles at me. I threw up my hands and froze. They kept me standing there with my hands in the air until the main body of troops arrived.

"The Red Army seemed less impressive at close range.

What I encountered was a column of infantry. No tanks, no trucks, no big guns. Just a company of open-faced men and boys led by two officers on horseback.

"The soldiers' khaki uniforms were dark with sweat. The packs on their backs looked heavy. Several horse-drawn wagons brought up the rear. I found out later they carried the company's food, tents and ammunition. *Impedimenta*, Caesar called it.

"Strange how the mind works in times of stress. I actually thought about Caesar and that infantry soldiering had not changed much since his time. But I digress.

"The two officers wore red epaulets and peaked caps. One was every inch the military man. He turned in his saddle and told his soldiers that they could break ranks and rest for a few moments. He seemed calm and at ease.

"The other officer seemed like a schoolteacher who had been plucked from his classroom without warning and dropped on top of a horse. He was as awkward and uncomfortable as his brother officer was strong and confident. A strange pair.

"Two soldiers searched me and found no weapon. They reported that to their captain. The two officers walked their horses up to where I stood. The sturdy officer half-saluted and told me, in Polish, that I could lower my arms. I thanked him in Russian and said I understood his language. He seemed relieved.

"The other officer, the slender one, said nothing, but he listened attentively while I told my story in ungrammatical

Russian. Both nodded in sympathy when I described the bombing of my village. Fortunately, I had learned the name of the place I saw destroyed.

"The officer with the military bearing wanted to know what he could expect to find on the road ahead. Not much, I told him. He seemed disappointed that I had seen no Polish troops in the countryside. No Germans, either. Only those three airplanes.

"The schoolteacher spoke up. 'Too bad you lost your papers,' he said. 'That always causes difficulties. But there will be some people coming along who will sort all that out. Until then, you will stay with us.'

"The other officer assured me that I was safe now. 'We will be pitching camp up ahead. You will spend the night with us and share our food.' He turned to the two soldiers who had searched me. 'Take care of him,' the officer told them. 'He's a good fellow who's had a run of bad luck.' True enough. I now found myself marching back west with the Red Army.

"The soldiers I walked with were youngsters, friendly and boisterous. They wore their caps at jaunty angles and talked loudly. The air was full of jokes, wise-cracks and complaints about the packs on their backs. They had been on the march for several days now, spoiling for their first fight. But, so far, there had been no opposition, no chance for a boy to test his courage.

"An hour before sunset, the infantry company left the road and moved into a field beside a small stream. Soldiers pulled tents from the wagons and set them up. Others busied themselves preparing the evening meal. I helped dig a latrine.

"After the simple evening meal, I was given a blanket and shown the tent where I was to sleep that night. So far, so good, I thought.

"Around dawn, I awoke to the roaring and clanging of a column of tanks and trucks moving past our camp. Bringing up the rear were two automobiles and a couple of small vans. They stopped and several officers got out.

"Maps were spread out on the hood of one of the cars. The officers, ours included, gathered around. When the conference ended, soldiers started setting up large field tents. Our company had been ordered to stay where it was for a while.

"The young officer who looked like a schoolteacher stood talking to one of the visiting officers, a short, older man with a large stomach. Another schoolteacher or a shopkeeper, I thought. They were deeply involved in their discussion, standing apart from the war, talking about more serious business.

"About an hour later, a soldier took me to one of the large field tents. Once inside, I saw that it was being used as an office as well as a place to sleep. Two cots were set up along one side of the tent, but most of the space was taken up by a folding table and several folding chairs. The schoolteacher and the shopkeeper greeted me courteously and addressed me by my false Polish name.

"The younger officer was a *politruk*, a political officer, assigned to the infantry company by the Communist Party to make sure the regular army officers performed their duties in accordance with correct Party principles.

"He was quite open in explaining this, although he did not use the word *politruk*, a slang word I learned only later. He told me that I was in luck. His superior officer had time to deal with my problem.

"The older man offered me a cigarette, then leaned back in his chair. How suddenly catastrophe can turn a man's life upside down, he remarked. He supposed he would hear more tales like mine as the Red Army encountered more refugees like me fleeing from the Germans.

"The Germans were not to be trusted, he said. That was the true reason the Red Army had crossed the Polish border. Sooner or later, he said, Hitler would look east and have to be stopped. Patriotic Poles, like me, might wish to join that fight.

"I agreed enthusiastically.

"The older officer told me I was fortunate. He handed me a printed form to read. It was written in Polish, very short, less than a page of type. There was a space to print my name, which I did.

"I can't remember the exact words, but the document stated that the petitioner sought entry to the Soviet Union where he intended to find the opportunity to work in his chosen profession. To this end, I sought the assistance of the Red Army and the Communist Party whose representatives I had approached, of my own free will, at this place and on this date.

"I could hardly believe what I was reading. The older officer leaned forward across the table. If the document correctly expressed my intentions, he would be pleased to witness my signature and I could be on my way to the Soviet Union within the hour.

"Well, of course, I signed the paper. My problem of crossing the Russian border had been solved by the Red Army itself.

"The shopkeeper countersigned the document and handed it to the schoolteacher. Then he got up from his desk.

"'So that is done,' he said. 'You can leave for Moscow right now, if you are ready.'

"I told him I was. 'Having lost everything,' I said with a laugh, 'I have nothing to pack.'

"The younger officer opened the tent flap and waved me outside with a smile. The three of us walked to the road where the vehicles were parked. The last in line was a small closed van, something like a delivery truck.

"The young officer opened the rear doors. 'It is not the most comfortable vehicle,' he said, 'but it is the best we have to offer. It will take you to a place where you can board a train.'

"I asked him if I would have trouble getting on the train. I had no papers, just the one I signed. Shouldn't I be carrying that paper with me?

"They both laughed at that. The young officer polished his spectacles. 'That document goes into your file,' the older one said. 'It is evidence, you see. Of espionage or worse. I only wish all such evidence was so easy to obtain.'

"'Oh, come now!' I cried. 'You can't be serious about this! I am not a spy! If you have any more questions, I'll try to answer them to your satisfaction!'

"I appealed to the younger officer, but he was no longer a kindly schoolteacher. His eyes had turned cold and he spoke through clenched teeth.

"He told me to just get in the truck. 'Quickly, now!'

"I saw his right hand move to the butt of the pistol on his hip.

"'Get in the truck,' he said, 'you fucking priest!'"

"GOOD LORD!" SAID FATHER Beck. "They knew!"

"Oh, yes," sighed Father Samozvanyetz. "They knew. And that staggered me. My knees buckled. I was barely able to hoist myself up into the van. I crawled in a ways, all crouched down, and looked back. The older one was grinning. 'Have a pleasant journey, priest!' he said. The younger one spat at me and slammed the van doors shut.

"There were no windows in the back of the van. I was alone in the darkness, holding on for dear life as we lurched along rough roads to some unknown destination."

Father Samozvanyetz stood up and paced slowly back and forth across the room.

"God forgive me," he said, "but suspicion darkened my mind and my soul. The Russians had known I was coming and had been waiting for me. But how was that possible? I had never planned to be on that road. I had happened upon that infantry company by chance. How could they have known I was coming?

"I tried to recall the people I encountered since leaving Rome. I scrutinized them with hatred and distrust! Saw their faces and despised them: the people in the villages who'd given me shelter, the men at the hotel in Warsaw, the clerk who assigned me my room, the sexton at the church, the customs inspector with the gold tooth who asked me to pray for Poland, the passport clerks, the train conductors, my fellow passengers, the household staff at the Russicum, even my Jesuit classmates! Perhaps some Jesuit had been captured and broken by the NKVD. Could that be it?

"The van stopped. The doors were flung open. I was dragged out into blinding sunlight, marched across a rail yard and thrown into an empty boxcar with a score of other unfortunates. Some of them tried to talk to me, but I shrank away and huddled in a corner. I sank deeper into myself, trying to identify my Judas Iscariot. Someone had betrayed me. Someone had told the NKVD that I was coming. Worst of all, someone had interfered with God's plan!"

Father Samozvanyetz pressed his forehead into the palm of his right hand.

"Such arrogance! As if I had the slightest inkling of God's plan!"

After a moment, he returned to his place at the table and sat down.

"Alex Samozvanyetz, Apostle to the Russians, cowered in that filthy boxcar, betrayed and forestalled, unmindful of the fear and suffering of those others riding to their own fates, poor souls to whom he might have provided some solace, some comfort. He could have served them as a priest, right then and there.

"The train rumbled on. But Alex Samozvanyetz, the Savior of Russia, could only see the thwarting of his holy mission. He couldn't see the opportunity to serve God so close at hand. No, he huddled in the darkness, a wounded beast, paralyzed with fear and self-pity.

"It was night when the train stopped and soldiers slammed back the boxcar doors. I climbed down and stood with the rest. We were in a railroad yard illuminated by spotlights on towers. Soldiers moved about, bells rang, steam engines shrieked, heavy machinery crashed and clanged all about us. The air was cold and damp. I was stiff from the long train ride and chilled to the bone. I head a voice call out: 'Samozvanyetz!' I couldn't believe my ears!

"Suddenly there was a face close to mine and a peaked officer's cap. 'You are Samozvanyetz.'

"It was not a question. It was a matter-of-fact statement. What could I say? I said, 'Yes.'

"Two armed guards marched me across the railroad tracks to another van. This van was black. The soldiers pushed me inside. The door slammed shut behind me. I stuck my fingers through the holes in the fence-like partitions and clung there.

"I tried to pray. But I could not. I was nothing more than a trapped and terrified animal. I had been caught and I knew what was ahead. In Rome, they had warned us. Now it was real: the inevitable questioning, the torture and, finally, the bullet in the back of the head. No, I could not pray. I was too frightened."

Father Samozvanyetz sat staring at something above and behind his listeners.

"The van stopped. The doors opened. I climbed out into the cold night air. My mouth was dry. My limbs numb. Spotlights flashed off cobblestones.

"I was trembling with fear in the courtyard of a large, dark building. I knew where I was. I knew that without being told. All my training had brought me to this place. Lubianka prison!

"Two men grabbed me by the armpits. They hustled me to a doorway and shoved me inside. I stumbled into blinding light. I lost my footing and plunged headlong down a flight of stairs."

Father Samozvanyetz closed his eyes.

"Please," he said. "May we stop now and continue tomorrow?"

CHAPTER · 10

IT RAINED THE NEXT DAY. A light, steady rain fell from leaden skies and formed small pools at the base of the trees. Herb Coogan detested this kind of soggy day. His sweater was no defense against the damp chill that had seeped into the retreat house. The conference room had a faint smell of mildew this morning and the wooden furniture felt clammy to the touch.

He walked to the kitchen where Brother Krause and Mitchell Sloane were toasting bread and scrambling eggs.

Coogan felt better after he got some food and hot coffee into his stomach. He went to the front door and looked out through the rain. The two Jesuits were approaching, black umbrellas over their heads, black raincoats over their cassocks. Their reflection, an odd black shape, slid ahead of them as they walked toward him along the glistening pavement.

Father Samozvanyetz seemed to be in a darker mood this dreary morning. He took his place at the head of the conference table.

"So, today, we talk about Lubianka," he said. "I must

confess that I was filled with dread during the night, knowing that I would be telling you about Lubianka this morning. That's how well the people there do their jobs. I don't suppose I was treated any differently upon arrival than any other prisoner, but it seemed that everything was designed to terrify and degrade me.

"To the eye, I suppose, Lubianka is not all that frightening. I never saw it from the outside, except for that glimpse from the courtyard. But I doubt that the building looks unusual. It was once a hotel, someone told me, and the hotel guest rooms had been made into cells. I don't know. It could be true, I suppose.

"The cell I occupied was bare, but clean. The offices where I was interrogated were furnished in the Old Russian style, somewhat Victorian. They reminded me of the visitors' parlors in our Jesuit houses: rugs on the floor, upholstered furniture, lamps with tassels on the shades. Perhaps that's what made the interrogations even more frightening."

Father Samozvanyetz drank some coffee and put his mug down on the table. He folded his hands on the table and leaned forward.

"So, what happened first?" he said. "When I fell down the stairs into the prison, two guards picked me up and dragged me down a corridor to a windowless room. There was no furniture. Nothing but a bare light bulb hanging from the ceiling, too high to reach. The guards slammed the steel door shut."

He closed his eyes and clenched his fists.

"Never had I heard anything so final! That terrifying sound of that door clanging shut. I almost emptied my bowels. I stood staring at the door paralyzed by fear. Would that cell door ever open again?

"God only knows how much later, the guards marched me to a photographer who took my picture, full face and profile. Then another man took my fingerprints. I almost wept as I watched him roll my thumbs and fingers across the paper. In the next room, a woman chopped off my hair and shaved my head bald.

"In another room, there were several more women in uniform. One told me to strip and give her my clothes. In Russian, I asked her why this was necessary. My clothes and I were to be disinfected, she told me. Prison rules.

"I looked about for a dressing room of some sort. The women laughed at me. 'Get on with it,' one said. 'Strip down and be quick about it. You've got nothing we haven't seen before.' They snatched my clothes away and tossed them into something that looked like a small furnace. I had nothing with which to cover myself.

"I was marched naked to the next room where I was sprayed with some sort of powdered chemical and then pushed into a shower and ordered to soap and rinse. The water was ice cold. There was no towel to dry myself. I was marched, naked and sopping wet, down another corridor and shoved into a bare cell just like the first one.

"I waited naked for a long time before being taken to

a dispensary where a female doctor examined me. The woman was quite professional, but I was humiliated and feeling utterly helpless. It was a relief to regain the privacy of a cell.

"No one bothered me for a long time. But no one fed me, either. Finally the cell door opened and a female guard handed me what was left of my clothes. She stood in the doorway and watched while I dressed.

"There wasn't much to put on. No underwear. No socks. No belt. The laces had been removed from my boots. Just my shirt and trousers, discolored by the heat of the disinfectant oven. But how grateful I was to put on those few clothes!

"I was supposed to feel gratitude, of course. I didn't know that. Not then. All I knew was that one moment I would be filled with feelings of gratitude and then be flooded with terror. It took a while to realize that I was being trained like an animal. But at the moment, I was just happy not to be naked.

"The female guard stepped aside when two men in military uniform entered the cell, the visors of their caps low over their eyes. I shrank back at the sight of their Sam Browne belts, their jackboots, the holsters on their waists. Was I going to be shot? Executed! But why did they have me put on clothes? There must be a rule against executing naked people.

"The men said nothing. They marched me down the corridor, one in front of me, the other behind. They took

me up several flights of stairs, then along a long dark hallway.

"We stopped. One of the uniformed men rapped on a
door, swung it open and waved me inside.

"I walked slowly across a carpet to a large desk. Seated
behind it was another man in uniform. An officer, I saw
by his epaulets. His tunic collar was unclasped. He wiped
a shock of hair from his broad forehead and stared at me
with bright blue eyes.

"He seemed too young for his office with its Victorian
furniture, the grave portraits of Lenin and Stalin on the
walls, the lamp with a stained glass shade that lit the surface of his ornately carved desk. The rest of the room was
in shadow.

"He gestured toward the plain wooden chair that stood
in front of his desk. 'Please sit down, Father Samozvanyetz,'
he said in English. 'I hope we can complete our business
without delay. I want to conclude all my cases as soon as
possible so that I can be posted to a military unit again.
War, I am sure you agree, is coming. There will be more
worthwhile things to do on the battlefield than behind this
desk. I'm sure you understand.'

"I said nothing. I was trying to get adjusted to my chair.
It was hard and difficult to sit on properly. I suppose it was
designed to be uncomfortable. 'You could be shot right
now, you know,' the young officer said. 'The charge against
you is espionage, after all. Please don't protest. I know very
well that you are not a spy. You are an American. You are a

Jesuit priest. You were trained in Rome to come to Russia to save souls. *Ad majorem Dei gloriam*, as you say in Latin. That's not espionage, of course. There are other sections of our criminal code that would apply, but I do not want to take the time to bend your case like a pretzel to fit those charges. I would rather prepare to defend Russia against the Nazis than to sit here and document your religious scheme. Do you understand what I am saying?'

"I did not and I told him so.

"'You may smoke, if you wish,' he said.

"I told him that I had no cigarettes. 'Too bad,' he said. 'They are hard to get here, too.'

"He lit a cigarette with a gold lighter and watched me watching him smoke.

"I was stunned, of course. It was obvious that he knew all about me. Everything. But how did he know what he knew? I did not dare ask.

"He rested his cigarette in an ashtray. 'Let me explain my position,' he said. 'And yours. Right now, I am in charge of your case. The Red Army officers who caught you know you are in custody. Some of our counter-intelligence officers also know, but nobody above the rank of colonel. The generals and their superiors will not be aware that I have you here until I file my report.

"'When they learn that I have a Jesuit in my possession, and an American to boot, they will order me to find out everything about your mission and your training. They will insist on my extracting every small detail, every little fact, before you are shot. That, unfortunately, is the way they are.

"'There is no changing them,' he sighed. 'And that means that I will have to spend weeks, months, perhaps even years, getting everything down on paper, just so. I will never get my transfer. The war will be fought without me.

"'On the other hand, I could report that the officers who apprehended you made an honest mistake. My investigation determined that you were not one of those Jesuits we are looking for, but just an ordinary Polish spy. You could confess to simple espionage tonight, sign the papers, and be shot without delay. That would be better for both of us, don't you agree?'

"I told him that I did not see how it would be better for me. He seemed surprised.

"'Why, I am offering you a quick ride to Heaven!' he said. 'Look at it this way. Within an hour, we could draw up a simple confession of espionage that would satisfy everybody: a Polish spy tries to get behind our lines and gets caught. You could sign it. We could have some tea and a few more cigarettes and enjoy some pleasant conversation. Later tonight, a bullet would send you straight up to Heaven to live happily ever after with that wonderful God of yours. I don't understand your hesitation. Isn't that your ultimate goal? To get to Heaven? Well, this very night, the angels and archangels and God Himself could be welcoming you and praising you! Saint Alex Samozvanyetz, the Holy Martyr! This very night!'

"Trying to make light of his proposal, I told him I understood his commendable desire for active duty and appreciated his sense of urgency. I, on the other hand, was in no hurry to be shot. I suggested that he just turn my case over to somebody else. He did not return my smile.

"'Where there's life, there's hope, eh? Is that what you are thinking? How wrong you are.' He paged through a folder on his desk. 'Let me assure you, Father Samozvanyetz, that your case is worse than hopeless. Someone else, someone who actually likes this kind of work, could use you to build a career. Your case could be investigated for years. That could be extremely painful. And it would all be the same in the end. A bullet in the brain.

"'You are much better off with me. I am offering you a quick way out. But you insist on buying time. Does that indicate a lack of faith on your part, Father Samozvanyetz? Could it be possible that you do not believe what you profess to believe?'

"I said nothing. How could I respond? I was clinging to life by my fingernails. He lit another cigarette and sat quietly, watching me.

"'You were involved in a foolish enterprise, Father Samozvanyetz. Personally, I think you should have an easy way out. Your superiors should have known that there was not the slightest chance of success. A brave man should not suffer because his superiors are stupid. At least, you were a brave man when you started out. Now, I am not so sure.'

"He sat quietly for several minutes and watched me squirm on that uncomfortable chair.

"'You are making a mistake not to accept my offer,' he said. 'I am not like the others here. I have no interest in destroying your faith. As far as I am concerned, you are what you are, you believe what you believe. But there are others here who delight in beating prisoners down to a level where they have no faith in anything, let alone God. It can be done, Father Samozvanyetz. It takes time, but they do it. And they enjoy doing it.'

"He let me sit and think about that for a while.

"'So, what do you say, Father Samozvanyetz? One shot and it is all over. Nothing more to worry about. Why not take my offer and leave this world with your faith intact?'

"I told him he was asking me to commit suicide. 'You must know that I can't do that,' I said.

He sighed and again brushed the hair from his forehead. 'I am asking you to be realistic,' he said.

"I told him I would rather take my chances with another officer.

"'You have too much faith in your faith,' he said. 'Or you are not listening to what I am saying. Are you not risking your immortal soul by hanging onto life? Aren't you risking eternal damnation? You can't withstand Lubianka. Nobody can. Look at yourself. Already you are the picture of despair, yet nothing serious has happened to you, yet.'

"He was right, of course. I sat there trembling on that odd, tormenting chair, knowing that everything he had said was all too true. What little strength I had was rooted in pride and arrogance. I could not expect to remain faithful under torture. Not for long. I could see that plainly and I was terrified. Was it better to get it over with quickly, as he said? He was waiting for my decision. But what could I say? What was right? What was wrong? I felt I had to say something.

"But I never got the chance. The young officer suddenly ran out of patience. 'This is getting me nowhere!' he said. He stood up and shouted for the guards standing outside the door: 'Get this man out of my sight!' With that, he stomped out of the office.

"I stood there bewildered. One of the guards grabbed me by the arm, spun me around and pushed me out the door. More stairs, another bleak corridor. The guards took me to another cell. I stayed in that one for a very, very long time."

Father Samozvanyetz left his chair and poured himself another mug of coffee. He walked to the window and looked outside.

"One gets the feeling that the rain will never stop," he said. "But it always does, doesn't it?"

"That young interrogator," said Herb Coogan. "Do you remember his name, by any chance?"

"I don't believe he ever told me his name. I never saw him again."

"Did you feel that he was just playing a game with you?"

"Not at the time," said Father Samozvanyetz. "I thought he was deadly serious. I think he was sincere about wanting to trade prison duty for the battlefield. That was probably true enough. But, later on, when I became used to the fear, I concluded that he never intended to have me shot that night. I am now sure his job that night was to start my emotional and moral breakdown. He successfully planted a seed of doubt in my mind that made me truly miserable."

"Any idea why?"

Father Samozvanyetz shrugged.

"Why, indeed?" he said. "I suppose the NKVD had something special in mind for me. But what that might have been, I have no idea. Whatever it was, I suppose it got lost during the war.

"Perhaps the people in charge of my case were assigned to more pressing duties. Perhaps the bureaucracy lost my files. I just don't know. But, for some reason, I did not go through the dehumanizing process he warned me about and that I heard about later in the camps. That is to say, I was not tortured, although the possibility of being tortured was never far from my mind.

"Mostly, I was left alone. Whether by accident or design, I was kept in isolation for a very long time. Perhaps that was intended to be a kind of torture. Who can say?

"Right at the beginning of my confinement, I lost all track of time. I hibernated. Vegetated. How can I describe it? I must have sunk into some sort of intellectual coma, completely without conscious thought. I was barely aware of the guards bringing food. I don't remember eating. Or bathing. Or using the latrine bucket, if there was one.

"How do I know that I went through this strange

comatose period? Only because I know that I survived it. Eventually, I was able to look back at it like a man who has emerged from a fog bank. But I can't tell you what was back there in the fog. Or how long I was in it. When it ended, it was like waking from a deep, troubled sleep, groggy and dazed, knowing that there had been terrible nightmares, but having no recollection of the dreams themselves.

"The first thing I became aware of was a sound that would come and go. I didn't know what it was. It was just there sometimes. And then, one day, I knew what it was. A bell in the distance. Soft. Faint. I could hear a bell tolling somewhere. A church bell? Perhaps. It sounded like a church bell.

"I began thinking about church bells. My bell tolled. Then it was silent. Then it tolled again. After a while, I realized that it tolled at regular intervals. That thought excited me. I began to wonder if I could put the bell to use in some way.

"It dawned on me that the bell might be marking the passing of time. Perhaps it marked each quarter hour. I sat up and listened. Soon, I was able to measure an hour, and then a complete day. Later, I was able to tell exactly how much time was passing.

"I began to study my surroundings. The door, the walls, the floor. My cell had a wooden floor much like the one in this room except that the wood was of better quality."

Father Samozvanyetz walked to the open space between the conference table and the windows of the room. He stepped off six paces.

"This," he said, "was the distance from the door to the wall opposite."

He walked to the windows, turned and took four paces toward the table. "This," he said, "is how wide the cell was, from wall to wall. The ceiling was about twelve feet high."

He walked back to the table where Herb Coogan was sketching a diagram on his yellow notepad.

"May I add to that?" he asked. Herb handed him the pad and pencil and Father Samozvanyetz sat down next to him.

"The door was here," he said, adding some lines to the diagram. "It was made of steel and it was locked and bolted from the outside. Right about eye level, there was a peephole with a cover that the guards swung aside when they wanted to look inside my cell. I could not move the cover from my side of the door, so I was not able to look outside into the corridor.

"Over here on this wall, directly opposite the door, was a large window frame with steel bars up and down, like this." He made a quick sketch on the pad. "There was no glass. The window had been covered, from the outside, by a sheet of tin so that no sunlight, or darkness either, could get into the cell. All illumination came from the bare light bulb hanging from the ceiling right above here. It stayed lit all the time, day and night.

"The four walls and the ceiling were covered with whitewash. On this wall, to the right as you face the door, in a recess behind a grill, there was a radiator that produced more noise than heat.

"Along the other wall was my bed. The head of the bed was flush up against the wall with the sealed window. It was a simple, wooden bed with a thin mattress, sheets, a pillow and a second blanket in winter. After a while, it was not too uncomfortable."

He drew a small circle in the corner of the room to the right of the door. "Over here," he said, "was the *parasha*, a bucket with a lid."

Father Samozvanyetz pushed the pad and pencil down the table to Herb Coogan. "Such were my accommodations at Hotel Lubianka," he said. "My guards were mostly women or old men. They kept changing. They were neither cruel nor kind. They were just businesslike, matter-of-fact, indifferent. They had orders not to speak to me any more than was absolutely necessary, and I did not try to tempt them into conversation.

"At first, it made no difference to me that women were watching me while I used the *parasha* or while I took a shower on those days when it was permitted. But, when I was coming back to life, the scrutiny of the female guards began to bother me. I realized that was a sign of progress. I had begun coming back when I realized that the bell somewhere outside the prison marked the passage of time. After I learned how to use the bell, I realized that time was a weapon the prison was using against me. You see?

"A prisoner was supposed to be only vaguely aware of time passing. He was to remain in his cell with its constant artificial light, to wonder when he would be released, to wonder when they would come for him, to wonder when he would be executed.

"Had I not discovered that my bell precisely marked the passage of each quarter hour, I might have drifted back into that limbo of fear and allowed my hours and days and weeks and months to slip away. That's the path to insanity that had been blocked by my bell.

"I got the idea that I could use it to make my own time. I could construct a life for myself quite apart from the life to which I had been condemned. I could use the bell to create and regulate a life no guard would be able to observe through a peep-hole."

Father Samozvanyetz looked at the quiet middle-aged man sitting to Coogan's left.

"I don't know how much you know about the Jesuit way of life, Professor Sloane. Quite simply, we're supposed to be both active and contemplative."

"Part minister, part monk," said Mitchell Sloane. "So I understand."

"Just so," said Father Samozvanyetz. "Jesuits strive to maintain a balance between activity and contemplation. That's something I was never able to do very well. So that young interrogator had easily caused me to fear not just death, but damnation. I had to admit that I was poorly prepared to face my uncertain future. Serving covertly as a priest in Russia, an active life for which I had trained so diligently was now an obvious impossibility. What I had to do now, to keep from going mad, was to embrace that very same contemplative life that I had so recklessly neglected. Now I was able to see that it was a matter of survival.

"I had been lax in my spiritual practice. But I remembered what I'd heard and read. Enough, at least, to know that my goal was attainable. Others had gone before me: Trappists and Carmelites, Cistercians, Poor Clares. They all had found a way to live an interior life. With God's help, so could I.

"Lubianka was never intended to be a monastery or a hermitage, but the prison routine and the penitential diet seldom changed. I didn't have to worry about what to eat or where to sleep or what to wear. All that had been decided for me. There was solitude and order.

"What I had to do was to accept my cell as my proper place in the world. It was there that I could spend my remaining days, be they many or few. I could spend them in frustration, fear and despair. Or I could spend them in fasting, prayer and meditation—*ad majorem Dei gloriam*.

"I had to convince myself that I hadn't been placed in my cell in Lubianka by the Red Army or the NKVD. I was not there because of a traitor's betrayal or some mistake of my own or by chance. It was God's will that I be where I was. I was right where I was supposed to be. God had placed me there for a reason.

"*Esse*. To be. I came to believe that 'to be' was my vocation.

"My first task was to study the prison routine and impose a monastic schedule upon it. Each morning at that same time, which I finally calculated was five-thirty, prison bells tolled and guards shouted me awake.

"I would rise, dress and make my bed while saying my morning prayers. The guard, most often a woman, would march me to the lavatory. It always smelled of carbolic acid. I would use the toilet, which was just a hole in the floor, and then wash myself in a large janitor's sink. You know the kind?"

He stretched out his arms. "A very big sink. In the same sink, I would wash out my *parasha*. Then, back to the cell. The church bell, which tolled just before I went to the lavatory, always tolled a few minutes after my return. Six o'clock. Time for my recitation of the Angelus.

"When the bell tolled at six-fifteen, I would begin my morning meditation. On the dot, not one minute before, not one minute after. I would stop when the bell tolled at seven-fifteen, even if I felt like continuing.

"Breakfast was served at seven-thirty. A guard would open the door and hand it to me. It was always the same. A piece of bread, always the same size and weight. Always a cup of boiling hot water with exactly one and one-half cubes of sugar. I could suck on the sugar or put it in the water. Always a big decision.

"I was allowed to sit on my bed to eat my meals. I always did so. And I always said Grace before and after meals. While waiting for the guard to return for my metal plate and cup, I would begin my preparation for Mass.

"I would start Mass at eight-fifteen and try to end at

eight-forty-five. Standing with my back to the peep hole, I recited the prayers I had committed to memory before leaving Rome. On what I believed to be Mondays, Wednesdays and Fridays, I would say the Mass in Latin. Tuesdays, Thursdays and Saturdays, I would follow the Russian Rite. Sundays were special. With the help of an imaginary choir, I would silently sing High Mass in Latin one week, in Russian the next.

"Then, after making my thanksgiving, I would go off with two companions for a long hike in the country. An imaginary *ambulatio*."

Father Samozvanyetz chuckled. "It was good to get out of the cell for a while. The weather was always the finest. Not too warm, not too cold. And I always had good company. At first, I didn't walk too far. Just up into the hills and back. And, at first, I only went out with people I knew, men with whom I had studied in the Society. But then I found new companions.

"One Sunday I would go hiking with Aristotle and Thomas Aquinas and listen to their ideas about God and Man. Other Sundays it would be General Grant and General Lee, Thomas Jefferson and George III, Francis Xavier and Francis of Assisi, Loyola and Lenin. I found I could walk with them as far as I wanted. I could hike to Niagara Falls, along the Nile, or along the Grand Canyon and still be home in time for the noon meal.

"Weekday mornings were a problem. At first I tried to fill them up with another meditation. But that was beyond my capabilities. I kept drifting off. So I decided to teach in a high school, which was a part of the Jesuit life I'd missed because of my special studies in Rome.

"Monday through Friday, after Mass, I would take a fifteen minute walk, six paces back and forth, to my imaginary high school where I taught Latin from nine to ten, mathematics from ten to eleven, Russian from eleven until noon. Most of my students were bright, but there were some slower ones who required special attention.

"At noon, while walking back to my cell, I would recite the Angelus. Then I would make my Examen, thinking over how I had used the day up to that point. The Examen was an important tool in my survival. It helped me keep a grip on reality. It was all very well to use my imagination to create some sort of interior life for myself, but I had to examine myself regularly to make sure that I was not beginning to believe that the creatures of my imagination were real.

"The mid-day meal was real enough, but not very substantial. The small bowl of fish soup was always delivered at thirty minutes after noon. It must have had some nutritional value, because I did not starve to death.

"I soon learned to save some bread from breakfast to mop up the bottom of the bowl. Sometimes there were a few small bones and a few pellets of grain. Every now and then, they gave us cabbage soup. The evening meal came just after the Angelus at six. The suppertime bowl would always contain four tablespoons of barley or lentils or kasha.

There would be another cup of hot water and the cube and a half of sugar. Not a grand meal but, once again, sufficient for a monk or a hermit.

"After the noontime meal, to get back to my schedule, I would walk around the novitiate grounds and silently recite fifteen decades of the Rosary using my fingers instead of beads, saying the prayers slowly and deliberately. One day I would pray in English, the next day in Latin, the day after that in Russian.

"When I finished, some of my brighter students would bring their chairs to my cell for my seminar on world literature. Together, we would examine in great detail every book that I could remember reading, and some I had only heard about. Sometimes, one of the authors whose work we were discussing joined our group. We always ended at four o'clock. Once everybody left, I would take a short stroll to clear my head and then spend another hour in meditation.

"At five-thirty, I would walk to the main chapel to join my fellow Jesuits for the recitation of the Litanies. And then, instead of joining the others in the refectory, I would return to my cell for supper.

"Every evening at seven o'clock I was taken for another walk, a real one this time, down the corridor to wash myself and clean out my *parasha*. Then I would be taken back to my cell. Time for recreation, just like relaxing with fellow monks in a monastery.

"To tell you the truth, I found this the most difficult part of my regimen. I knew recreation was important.

The mind needs to relax, as does the body. Otherwise, it will break down. But I had nothing to relax with except my mind. Idle daydreaming, I feared, might be too risky. It seemed safer to recall as many actual recreation periods as I could.

"I began with the last one in Rome and worked my way back into the past. It didn't matter if I couldn't reconstruct specific conversations or remember the content of the puns and jokes. Sometimes, I did. But it was enough to recall the camaraderie and the laughter.

"I found it a good idea to close out my recreation periods with music. Sometimes we'd have a community sing. A silent one, of course. Sometimes we'd put some records on the phonograph and listen to a band concert or a symphony.

"Recreation ended precisely at nine o'clock. Prisoners had to be in bed by ten. I would use that final hour to make another Examen, prepare my points for my morning meditation and say my nighttime prayers. I went to bed at ten o'clock on the dot.

"And that," said Father Samozvanyetz, "was how I spent the next two years."

Herb Coogan chewed on his pencil for a moment and then said: "Saturday. You didn't tell us what happened on Saturdays."

Father Samozvanyetz smiled. "Sports," he said. "Baseball in the summer, football in the fall, hockey in the winter, basketball in the spring. Very orderly. But towards the middle of football season in 1941, by my reckoning, things began to change.

"I began to hear sirens wailing outside the prison. I thought, for the first few nights, that I was just hearing air-raid drills, like the ones we had been having in Rome before I left. And that probably was true, at first.

"Mind you, I had heard no news of any kind since my imprisonment, so I had no way of knowing that the war between Russia and Germany had begun. Nor did I know that most of the prisoners in Lubianka were being evacuated. And only much later, when I was in the camps, did I learn just how close the German armies had come to Moscow.

"In October of 1941, an approximate date I was able to determine only much later, I was moved to a cell in the basement of Lubianka. I could no longer hear the sirens and I could no longer hear my church bell. Nor could I hear the war when it approached Moscow. But I could feel it.

"Down in the bowels of the prison, I knew when the bombing began. I could hear nothing, but the walls and floor of my cell shuddered. The very foundations of the building vibrated with greater or lesser intensity depending on how close the bombs and shells exploded. It was terrifying to cower there and feel the impact without having any idea of what was really going on outside.

"There were other prisoners in the cellar. I never saw them, but I could hear them. At least, I thought I could.

From time to time during the air raids, I would hear cries of fright. But the sounds were very faint and I thought, at first, that I might be imagining things.

"The guard I saw most often was an old man with a full white moustache who brought me my food in the evening and again in the morning. He looked like he might have been a sergeant-major in the Czar's army. During the bombing or shelling, he had a positively ferocious demeanor. His eyes would flash with a war-like glare when he handed me my food and his moustache would bristle. But he was never unkind.

"One night, when the bombardment felt especially heavy, he actually spoke to me. The old man, his eyes blazing, marched into my cell to retrieve my bowl. The cellar walls were quaking from the explosions. He said nothing, as usual, until he was leaving. He glanced up and down the corridor and then spoke in a savage whisper. 'Stalin is in Moscow!' he said proudly.

"With that, he grinned and closed the cell door. I realized he was trying to give me the courage to endure the terrors of the night. Did he do the same for the other prisoners? I don't know. I suppose he did. And it was indeed a bad night. The bombing lasted longer and seemed heavier than usual. But the old man served breakfast at the usual time, according to regulations.

"The old sergeant-major entered my cell that morning more bellicose than ever. 'Courage!' he whispered to me. 'God will protect us here. Moscow shall not fall!'

"Quite impulsively, I whispered back. 'God bless you for the gift of bread, my brave sergeant,' I said. 'Listen carefully. I am a priest. If I also had a thimbleful of wine and a fragment of bread, I could say Mass tonight for Holy Mother Russia.'

"His eyes widened. He stumbled backwards out of my cell, slammed the door shut and shot the bolt with great force. I sank to the floor, bitterly disappointed.

"But that evening, when the sergeant-major delivered my bowl of barley soup, my cup of hot water and my sugar, he gave me a small piece of bread and another cup with a small amount of wine. 'I have told those I trust that you will say Mass tonight, Reverend Father,' he said. 'Listen for my signal. I will knock on your door three times when it is safe. Rap twice when you are about to begin and I will tell the others to start their prayers.'

"And so, thanks to that guard, I was able to offer the holy sacrifice of the Mass in the cellar of Lubianka surrounded by my unseen congregation. And not just that night, but on all those other nights when Moscow was under attack until early December, I think it was, when I was taken out of the cellar. I never saw that faithful old sergeant-major again.

"I was returned to the very cell I had been in before, thank goodness, back to my bell and to my monastic routine. I don't think the authorities ever learned of my underground Masses. At least, it was never mentioned in any subsequent interrogations. There were eight of them all told, quite routine, each one less frightening than the last.

"Except for those sessions with the interrogators, I spent the rest of my time in Lubianka alone in that self-same cell. I have tried to calculate how long I was there. Not counting that initial comatose period when I had no sense of time, or the fifty-five days in the cellar during the bombing, I reckon that I was in solitary confinement for 1,934 days."

"That would be a little over five years," said Mitchell Sloane.

"Just so." Father Samozvanyetz took a deep breath. "I believe we would all like some water now, if you would be so kind, Brother Krause."

HERB COOGAN SAT LISTENING to the rain beating against the retreat house windows. Brother Krause brought a pitcher of water and some glasses to the table. Herb took a few swallows and wiped his mouth with his hand. Mitchell Sloane caught his attention and Herb followed his eyes to the other side of the table where Father Beck sat, lost in thought. He looked back at Sloane and shrugged. He couldn't tell what his old teacher had heard or what he was thinking.

After the lunch break, Mitchell Sloane took Herb Coogan aside "What do you make of it so far?" he asked. "Father Beck seems to have heard something this morning that I didn't hear."

"It all sounded credible to me," said Coogan. "Father Beck seemed really impressed by the priest's story, but you may be right."

"Maybe it was something that didn't ring true about the religious stuff, you think? You'd know better than me, Herb. You're a church-going Catholic, right? That's not my area of expertise, to say the least."

"I'm not an expert, but everything he told us about his spiritual experience made sense to me. His circumstances were unusual, but I wasn't surprised by the way he said he coped with them. It all seemed logical and, I guess I have to call it, very Catholic."

"So maybe it's something else. I think it's time to shake him up a bit this afternoon."

CHAPTER · 11

"THERE'S NOT MUCH MORE to tell about Lubianka," said Father Samozvanyetz. "In mid-April of the sixth year of my imprisonment, I was taken from my cell during the middle of the night and escorted to an interrogation parlor where an officer I had never seen before handed me a document to read. He told me it was the judicial verdict in my case.

"With his permission, I sat down and read through the papers. It was a momentous occasion for me, so I remember what I read very clearly. The document said that I had been found guilty of the charges brought against me under Article 58:10 of the Criminal Code. I was, therefore, sentenced to fifteen years at hard labor. I asked the officer for an explanation of the charge against me.

"He told me that Article 58:10 dealt with any propaganda or agitation containing an appeal to overthrow, undermine or weaken the Soviet regime. It specifically prohibited what was described as 'exploitation of the religious prejudices of the masses.'

"The officer said, 'Fifteen years is not so bad. Better than being shot for espionage, wouldn't you say? I congratulate you on your good fortune. It is better to walk out of Lubianka, no matter what your destination, than to be carried out.'

"I had to agree with him, of course. He then instructed me to sign the document to show that I understood the charges and accepted the verdict as just.

"When I hesitated, he laughed. 'The signature will either be in your handwriting or mine,' he said. 'You really have no decision to make.' So, I signed it.

"I did not return to my cell. Two guards entered and escorted me from the room, along some corridors, down some stairs and out into the floodlit courtyard. I was put in the back of a closed prison van. And so I left Lubianka, just as I'd arrived, in the dead of night. The date, I believe, was April 14, 1945."

Father Samozvanyetz rubbed his hands together.

"Well, that's it," he said. "What else can I tell you about Lubianka, gentlemen?"

Mitchell Sloane paged through his notes. "I would like to know more about your interrogations," he said without looking up. "I believe you said there were eight in all?"

"Yes, there were eight. The first you know about."

The priest took a sip of water.

"What can I tell you about the others?" he said. "They were more or less pointless, as far as I was concerned. We covered no new ground. They just seemed to want me to agree with their understanding of my case, that's all."

"Were you interrogated on any sort of schedule?"

"None that I could determine. My best guess would be that the prison administration changed from time to time. When it did, I suppose, my case would be reviewed. The interrogations became shorter and less detailed. Judging from the cursory way the last few were conducted, I had become increasingly insignificant in the general scheme of things. A small fish, really."

"Were you at any time subjected to physical torture?"

"No, I was not. The officers tended to be verbally abusive at times, but the interrogations were conducted in a businesslike manner."

"Did you ever try to mislead your interrogators?"

"No, I told them the truth."

Father Samozvanyetz looked around the conference table.

"I told them the truth," he said again. "What harm could it have done? They knew everything about me and about the Society's Russian mission. I never saw the contents of the files to which they referred, but it was apparent that the NKVD had assembled a voluminous dossier. They must have been accumulating information for years and, judging from the questions they asked, everything they had learned about our training and our intentions was accurate. Even so, every now and then, it had to be gone over again, point by point."

"Did any of your interrogators tell you anything about other Jesuits they might have apprehended?"

"Nothing specific."

"What do you think?"

"I think they caught all of us. That's the impression I got, although they said nothing directly."

"What do you think happened to the others?"

"I don't know. I can only speculate. My interrogators never asked me for information about their whereabouts. So I have to conclude that they knew where all of them were. Which is to say, they knew they were all dead. Executed."

"Might they not have been in prison or in the labor camps?"

"Perhaps, but I don't think so."

"Why not?"

"Had they been alive somewhere, I would have heard something about them over the years. The camps are full of rumors and stories and legends. The only story I ever heard was about a mysterious priest who said Mass in the cellars of Lubianka during the darkest days of the Great Patriotic War. That, of course, was me."

Mitchell Sloane stared at his notepad and waited.

"No," said Father Samozvanyetz, "I never heard one word about any other Jesuits in Russia. I listened carefully, I assure you. I'm convinced that they were all caught soon after entering the Soviet Union. I doubt that they ever came in contact with any Russian civilians. Otherwise, I think, I would have heard something. No, I think they were all caught and shot."

"But you were not executed."

"No, I was not. I think the war had a lot to do with that. According to the convicts I met in the camps, the State became less rigorous about suppressing religious practices when the Germans attacked Russia. Stalin, they said, was desperate enough to accept the help of any ally, even God. That shift in policy might have been what saved me.

"My interrogators at Lubianka never seemed to know what to do with me. They knew that I wasn't a German spy and I doubt that anybody saw me as a serious threat. I eventually became a nagging bureaucratic problem, I suppose. A clerical error, you might say."

"Ever wonder why the NKVD didn't correct their clerical error by simply eliminating the cleric?"

"There was certainly nothing to stop them. But they did not. Obviously, God had other plans for me. That's the only explanation I can give you."

"I suppose it will have to do, for the moment."

Mitchell Sloane toyed with his papers, then looked up at the priest.

"Please forgive me, but my job is dealing with facts."

"So is mine," said Father Samozvanyetz.

CHAPTER · 12

THE SKIES OVER SOUTHERN Ohio had cleared during the night. The sun was bright and mist rose from the novitiate's lawns. Inside the retreat house, Herb Coogan and Mitchell Sloane were spreading a large map of the Soviet Union across the conference table. They placed empty coffee mugs at the map's four corners to hold it down.

"It seems odd to be exploring Siberia on such a warm spring morning," said Father Samozvanyetz.

He studied the map for several minutes. "Impressive, Professor Sloane. You know more about Siberia than the people who live there."

"We're wondering how accurate it is," said Sloane.

"It certainly seems to be accurate. I am surprised that there is so much detail."

He tapped the map with his finger. "Right around here, there are supposed to be nomad tribes that practice cannibalism. That is a tall tale the guards tell to scare the convicts, but it's true that they pay nomads a bounty for bringing in escaped prisoners. Dead or alive."

"Do many prisoners try to escape?"

"Not many. What would be the point? Where would they go?"

He shrugged and bent over the map again. "Let's see if I can show you where I've been."

He pointed to the railroad line his boxcar had traveled. His finger moved north out of Moscow, then northeast to Kotlas.

"There was a camp near this town where I was kept for several months before being sent farther north, by boxcar again, to the Pechora River valley. The Pechora is a broad river. Much bigger than the Ohio. I met Muscovites in the camps who said they'd never before known of its existence. See how it bends around to the north and empties into the Barents Sea?

"Right around there, where the river makes this huge horseshoe, there are several labor camps. It's an immense area and this is where I served my sentence. In three different camps, all of them much the same."

His finger roamed southwestward over the map.

"After I was paroled, I was given a job and a place to live, right here, at the state farm where that American found me."

"Like finding a needle in a haystack," said Sloane.

"Yes, exactly. Amazing, isn't it? You can see how miraculous it was that he found me there in the middle of nowhere."

"Yes," said Mitchell Sloane. "It's amazing, all right."

Father Beck arrived slightly out of breath.

"What's amazing?" he asked as he joined the group at the table.

"Father Samozvanyetz was showing us where he'd been in Siberia," said Brother Krause. "Three labor camps up here and then down here at the farm where Mister Hoffmann found him."

"We were saying how it was amazing, considering the vast distances," said Sloane. "Miraculous, even."

"Well, miracle or coincidence, it happened, didn't it?" said Father Beck.

"Yes, there's no denying that they met," said Sloane. He began rolling up the map. "I hate to give Siberian geography short shrift, Father Samozvanyetz, but we'd better press on."

He slid a rubber band around the rolled map and took his place at the table. "You don't have to describe the Soviet penal system in any great detail. We know a lot about it from other sources. Can we assume that your camp experience was typical?"

"Physically? Yes, you can assume that."

"We know the camps are used to isolate enemies of the State, real or imagined. We know the life expectancy of the prisoners is short."

"In many cases, that is correct."

"But you survived for fifteen years," said Sloane. "How do you account for that?"

"For one thing, I come from peasant stock. My body has been sturdy and I never had any serious illnesses. I don't feel pain as acutely as slender men like you or Father Beck. Brother Krause and I are built to take a lot of punishment, right?"

Brother Krause nodded in agreement.

"Also," the priest said, "I believe that deliberate thinking is necessary to survive and my mind plods from A to B to C to D. Slow but sure. It doesn't take leaps. And, I have to say, Lubianka prepared me to survive mentally. And, if you'll forgive me, spiritually."

Mitchell Sloane did not comment. Nor did he write anything down.

"Then I had something the other convicts didn't have," said Father Samozvanyetz. "My vocation. For me, being sent to the camps was not punishment. It was a chance to do the job I had been trained to do. I went to Siberia in a good frame of mind.

"The good weather helped me. I left Lubianka in the springtime. Siberia was not that cold when I got there. The tundra was thawing. The ground was soggy and boglike. I saw shrubs and wild flowers blooming. But the days grew longer and longer until the sun never set at all. By mid-summer, the mosquitoes made me long for the first killing frost.

"It was a good while before the temperature began to drop. It fell gradually, not all of a sudden. Each day was shorter and colder than the one before. The wind grew stronger day by day. Snow started to fall gradually until the ground was completely covered. Finally, there was the long polar night with the bitter cold, and winds that swept across the snow and struck men dead. But not me, thank God, because I had been given a chance to ease into the Siberian winter.

"It was a hard life. I was always hungry, but I was never beaten by the guards or robbed by other convicts. It was construction work that we were involved in, mostly. The chances for injury were great. Laboring long hours in the cold, the mind slows down, the hand loses its grip, and then there's an accident, very often fatal.

"That happened to others, but not to me. I was never seriously injured because I watched my step and obeyed the rules. And not just to survive, but to be of service to others. But why was I spared, Professor? God protected me. That's what I believe. But maybe 'mind over matter' would be an easier explanation to accept?"

Sloane did not look up from his yellow pad. "You said yesterday that you heard nothing about any other Jesuits. Did you meet or hear about any other Americans?"

"No, I did not. I heard rumors, but I never met anyone who'd actually seen an American in the camps. No doubt there were some, but I never heard anything specific. No names. Just vague references and nothing more. I listened carefully to such idle talk, but I learned nothing concrete."

"I'm not clear about your own status in the camps," said Sloane. "Did they know you were an American?"

"The commandant at the first camp did. I know that because we discussed it when I arrived from Lubianka. After that, it wasn't mentioned. Perhaps it was forgotten. The guards and the other convicts took me for Russian. I never gave them any reason to think otherwise."

"Were they aware that you were a priest?"

"I'm sure the officials knew. Well, at least, the first commandant did. I assume it was in my records. But then, again, I was never allowed to examine my file."

"How about the other prisoners?"

Father Samozvanyetz was slow to answer.

"I was careful to keep my identity secret," he said.

"Convicts inform on each other to obtain special favors or extra rations, God forgive them. So, as far as the guards and the other convicts were concerned, Alex Samozvanyetz was just another *zek*. Another convict. I did what I could for the dying, but very secretly.

"I don't know what the others thought about my spending so much time with men who were close to death. But I don't think they suspected that I was a priest. I was never turned in, at any rate."

Father Samozvanyetz stopped speaking and stared straight ahead.

"I am on the edge of some very dangerous ground here," he said quietly. "I don't mind telling you what I went through myself. But about the people in the camps? That's another matter. I want to cooperate as best I can, but I'm afraid to trust my memory now.

"You see, I know a lot about a lot of people. But how much did I learn when we were working side by side, when they did not know I was a priest? And how much did I learn when they were making their death-bed confessions?"

Father Beck stood up. He walked to the head of the table and stood beside Father Samozvanyetz.

"We'd better move on to something else," he said. "You know that a priest may not discuss anything he has heard during a confession. He just can't talk about it. Do we all understand that?"

"We understand, Father," said Coogan.

Professor Sloane sighed and flipped rapidly through several sheets of his legal notepad.

"Perhaps we can talk about this," he said. "Were you ever given any indoctrination? In private or in a group?"

"Never privately," said Father Samozvanyetz. "Except for that first interrogator at Lubianka, no one in authority seemed to care what I thought about Communism. No one ever tried to convert me."

"How about in a group?"

"Only once. The commandant of the second camp I went to staged a series of lectures to aid in what he called our 're-education.' We would assemble outdoors and be harangued by a young officer standing on a wooden platform. A month or so of boring lectures on Marx and Lenin and so forth. Then, I guess, someone told the commandant that his job was to get the work done, not to make us good Communists."

"Do you recall any period of time when you might have been unconscious?"

"Apart from sleeping, you mean? When I wasn't asleep, I was conscious."

"Never knocked unconscious by a blow to the head? On the job? In a fight?"

"No."

"Anaesthesia in a hospital or at the dentist?"

"I never saw a hospital or a dentist. But, no, I never had any anaesthesia."

"Ever given a sedative to make you sleep?"

"No."

"Ever pass out from the use of drugs or alcohol?"

"No."

"When you described those first days at Lubianka, you said you were in something like a comatose state. You had no sense of time passing."

"Comatose may be too strong a term. I was deeply depressed, of course. Numb."

"You knew who you were, where you were, what was happening?"

"I knew what was happening. I didn't care. But I knew."

"Do you recall any other long periods like that?"

"No, that was the only one."

"Looking back over the years, are you aware of any gaps in your experience?"

"I don't understand."

"Did you ever feel you had lost a few hours, or a day, or maybe a week? Did you ever think that it was Wednesday, for example, and then realize that it was really Friday?"

"Well, I didn't have a calendar, so I didn't always know precisely what day it was. I probably made many errors about the specific day or date. But I don't recall ever having the feeling that you describe."

"Today always followed yesterday?"

"Oh, yes," said the priest. "And tomorrow always followed today. Even if I happened to give them the wrong names."

"So you're not aware of any breaks or gaps in the passage of time?"

"That's correct," said Father Samozvanyetz. "Perhaps I could be more helpful if I knew what you're looking for."

"I'm looking for any substantial period of time that you can't account for when someone could have tampered with your mind. You wouldn't be aware of what went on in such a blank period, of course, but you might be aware of the gap in time itself."

"You think I might have been hypnotized?"

"Or drugged. Something like that."

"That seems a bit far-fetched, but I suppose such a thing could happen."

Father Samozvanyetz frowned and tapped the edge of the table with his forefinger.

"The life of a convict is monotonous in the extreme," he said quietly, not looking up. "One day blends into another and also the months and the years, so that it's hard to distinguish one from another. But I think that, if you had the time and the patience to listen, I could probably reconstruct each and every day in order. It would be a long string of mostly uninteresting events. But, yes, it would be continuous."

He looked the professor in the eye.

"I think that if something was missing, some gap in time, as you put it. it would be apparent to me. Something like a big hole in a highway. But I am aware of nothing like that. It was not a pleasant road I travelled, but there were no empty spaces in it."

Mitchell Sloane leaned forward in his chair.

"I'd like to get clear on something, Father, since the matter of death-bed confessions has been brought up."

He raised his hand to ward off Father Beck's objections.

"I understand that priests are not allowed to reveal what they hear in confession, that you can't talk about any of that. But could we talk around it? I'm sure that certain questions are going to be raised in Washington."

"Then we'd best discuss them now," said Father Samozvanyetz. "Perhaps I am scrupulous about the Seal of Confession, but I don't think so. I feel that I am in great danger and I would appreciate your understanding.

"I didn't have much practical experience as a priest before I was sent to Russia. I heard confessions in Rome after my ordination, but not all that many. And, during my confinement, I had no other priests to talk to about this problem of memory, for example. Not until now. Do priests remember what they hear in confession, John?"

"I suppose it depends on the priest," said Father Beck.

"I've usually forgotten what I've heard by the time I leave the confessional booth. Most sins aren't memorable. Just human, commonplace, a bit dreary. Sometimes I recall the mood of a penitent, but nothing specific, really. I wouldn't call that remembering, exactly. It's more like retaining a general impression. But that's just me. I can't speak for other priests."

"That's how it was with me in Rome," said Father Samozvanyetz. "After hearing confessions, there would remain only the recollection of having heard recitals of human weakness and personal failure. So it was easy to listen and absolve and then forget. But then Mussolini never entered my confessional. Nor any of his Fascist thugs."

"Yes, that would have been something any priest would remember," said Father Beck.

"Unfortunately, John, I haven't been able to forget anything I heard in the camps, just as I remember everything I saw. Memory helped me survive Lubianka. In the camps, it was my greatest enemy."

He turned to Mitchell Sloane and smiled.

"I'm afraid we can't escape the subject of faith, can we? But you must understand that I can't escape my beliefs. It's relevant, I think you'll agree. In the camps, it was much harder to keep my faith intact than it ever was in Lubianka.

"Every day I witnessed the cruelty that human beings inflicted on other human beings. Not inflicted by animals or devils, but by obedient men just following orders.

"Alone in Lubianka, it wasn't difficult for me to discern

and accept God's will for me. But accepting the suffering of others? That was an entirely different matter. The great temptation in the camps was to lose faith, not only in God, but also in Man. Day after day, year after year, I saw cruelty and despair. Men maimed and broken in spirit. I was powerless to give them any solace in religion, not overtly.

"I had to survive. To survive, I had to remain silent and not resist. How could a dead priest help anyone? And so I stood mute and absorbed one shock after another, numbed by my daily observation of cruelty.

"I knew that if I lost faith in Man, I would soon lose faith in God. And so I prayed that God would make me understand that what I was witnessing was somehow a manifestation of His will. That prayer has yet to be answered."

Father Samozvanyetz poured himself half a glass of water and drank it down.

"What I did come to accept is this: it was God's will that I be removed from the civilized world and be taken to the very brink of Hell where I had no choice but to look helplessly into the abyss and witness the agonies of the damned. I accepted the fact that it was God's will that I stay there to offer spiritual comfort to dying convicts. To do that, I had to listen to them. To be a clandestine chaplain, if you will.

"What can I say about those men? Some of their names might be familiar to you, were I free to utter them. High-ranking political and military men who had fallen out of favor with Stalin and been cast into the Pit. I dare not be more specific.

"But I can say that I ministered to many such men as they were dying. Some cursed me and rejected my help. Others fought for their souls during their last moments on this earth and spoke the truth."

Father Beck watched his friend get up from his chair and walk across the room to a window and stare out across the lawn, his eyes fixed on some distant horror that only he could see.

"Dear God," murmured Father Samozvanyetz. "What awful truths they told!"

He turned, appealing for understanding.

"They were not demons. They were men, just like us. Some had been men of faith once. Devout, you might even say. Some had been idealists: they'd set out to do what was right and just. But what they believed so fervently turned on them, corrupted them, betrayed them and, in the end, condemned them to die in the midst of cruelty and depravity and despair. That some of them, even a handful, were able to grasp desperately for God's forgiveness at the end? That was indeed miraculous.

"But most could not. They were too deeply buried in their hatred of God and Man and Self. But even some of those damned souls talked to me at the end. They were not looking for forgiveness, but just vomiting out their dreadful life stories.

"Oh, I gave them all absolution, even those who cursed me and cursed God. I could only trust in God's infinite mercy. But each time I recited the words of absolution,

I found my own faith tested. For I had to wonder: could even God truly forgive what I was forced to hear?

"As a priest I am bound by the Seal of Confession. But am I condemned to remember what I was told by all those dying men? I yearn to share that burden, but I know that to unburden myself, now or in the future, would be to risk eternal damnation. So I must carry this burden to my grave alone, unless God answers my prayers and purges it all from my memory.

"So far, that does not seem to be God's will for me."

Father Beck reached out to Mitchell Sloane.

"Must we continue this line of questioning, Professor?"

"No, I think I've heard enough." Sloane made a show of gathering up his notes and putting them in order. "There's just one loose end I'd like to tie up, Father Samozvanyetz, if you don't mind. Your letter to the United States. When did you decide to write it?"

"I wrote my letter in a burst of optimism. My sentence had been served. I was on parole. I had arrived at a state farm where a job was waiting for me. I really felt I was a free man. So, I thought, why not? Nothing ventured, nothing gained. I'll write a letter to my Provincial, whoever that might be, and let him know where I am. Maybe he can make arrangements to bring me home. It seemed a reasonable thing to do at the time.

"I tried to mail my letter, but there was no post office. I realized then that it did not matter what my release papers stated. I was by no means free. Siberia still held me prisoner.

"I kept the letter in my toolbox, not because I thought I would ever have the opportunity to send it, but as a souvenir of my naïveté. I could have torn it up and thrown it away. But, had I done that, I think I would have thrown my life away as well.

"So I kept that fragment of hope inside my toolbox to remind me that all might not be lost. Time passed. And then, one fine day, a lone American walked into the shed where I was working. I couldn't believe my eyes!

"And what was more miraculous, I ask you? That this American should stumble across me in the middle of Siberia? Or that I had my letter ready and waiting for him to carry back to the United States?"

Father Samozvanyetz threw up his hands.

"But that is what happened. Was it chance? Or was it God's will? You can believe what you want to believe, but one fact cannot be denied, Professor Sloane. I am here."

"Yes," said Sloane. "You are here. Now the question is: What's to be done with you?"

"May I make a suggestion?" said Father Beck. "If you have no more specific questions, perhaps we should just adjourn and maintain the status quo. Father Samozvanyetz can stay here indefinitely until the government makes its decisions. Any objections?"

There were none.

CHAPTER · 13

IT TOOK BROTHER KRAUSE a full day to deal with the work that had piled up on his desk during his stay at Milford. When he got around to typing up his transcript of the debriefing, he found something worth mentioning to the Provincial.

"That church in Warsaw, Father Novak? Father Samozvanyetz says he saw red vestments laid out in the sacristy for Mass the next morning. Red vestments for the feast day of a martyr, something he says he didn't want to become. Well, I did some research. The Germans announced that von Ribbentrop was flying to Moscow on August 21, 1939. Father Samozvanyetz says he heard that news at the Warsaw train station that afternoon, before he went to that church. That puts put him there the night of the 21st. The red vestments would be for Mass the next morning: August 22. I checked the *Missale Romanum*. Looks like vestments from August 19 through 23 would have been white, not red."

"Or they could have been black," said Father Novak. "A Mass for the Dead can be said on any weekday, no matter what feast day it is."

"Right. White or black, but not red. Take a look."

He put the Roman Missal on the provincial's desk and began turning pages.

"August 19: Saint John Eudes, white vestments. August 20: Saint Bernard, white. August 21: Saint Jane Francis de Chantal, white. August 22, the day in question: Octave of the Assumption of the Blessed Virgin, white vestments. There are no red vestments until August 24: Saint Bartholomew, Apostle and Martyr. So Father Samozvanyetz couldn't have seen red vestments when von Ribbentrop was in Warsaw."

"Maybe the parish priest or his sacristan made a mistake," said Father Novak. "Or, wait a minute! There's another possibility. There's a second entry for August 22. It's also the feast of Saints Timothy, Hippolytus and Symphorian, Martyrs. That could account for the red vestments. The pastor could have chosen to say a Red Mass instead of a White Mass."

"Why would he do that?"

"Maybe the priest's name was Timothy. Or maybe Timothy was his confirmation name."

"In Warsaw?" said Brother Krause. "Maybe I'm wrong, but I don't think Polish parents would name a boy Timothy or that any Polish kid would choose it when he got confirmed."

"Well, you can check that out easily enough," said Father Novak. "We're in Chicago, remember?"

*   *   *

BROTHER KRAUSE SPENT A productive half-hour at St. Mary of Czestochowa's rectory in Cicero looking over some maps of pre-war Poland with one of the older parishioners, a Polish-American woman who had immigrated to the United States in 1937. Born and raised in Warsaw, she had no trouble pointing out the train station and church across the street from the park that Father Samozvanyetz had described.

"That was my parish," she said proudly. "I went to grade school there."

She remembered the pastor, Monsignor Teodor Piasecki. He had died several years after the war, she said, but the church was still there. She knew that from letters she received from her cousin who still lived in Warsaw.

Brother Krause asked if, by any chance, she also knew Monsignor Piasecki's confirmation name.

"Who could forget? He was so proud of it. Every year, he celebrated a special Mass for us school children and gave a sermon all about this Roman martyr whose name he took when he was confirmed. And then he gave us children the rest of the day off from school. We always looked forward to Saint Symphorian's Day. So I remember it well."

BROTHER KRAUSE RETURNED TO the office and told Father Novak what he'd learned. Then he phoned Herb Coogan and gave him the name and location of the church in Warsaw. Coogan passed it on to Mitchell Sloane in Washington.

"That's great," said the professor. "That's the last fact I had to nail down. Everything else seems to check out. The descriptions of Lubianka and the prison camps are accurate. The references to times and places and historical events also check out. Nothing I've heard from our people in Moscow contradicts anything he told us. For example, it would indeed be possible to hear a bell from a clock tower inside Lubianka, depending on where his cell was located."

"How about his time in Poland?"

"The hotel where he said he spent the night in Warsaw couldn't be found. There had been a few that fit the description, but they were destroyed during the war. The village he saw being bombed when he was walking east along the country roads? It was never rebuilt, but the ruins are still there. And the terrain in that area is still pretty much like he described it, our people say. No discrepancies, so far. All I have to do now is get someone from the embassy to check out that church crypt."

THE NEXT MORNING, A young man and young woman who worked at the U.S. Embassy in Warsaw went to Mass at the church Brother Krause identified. The pastor was kind enough to let them take photographs of the crypt beneath the main altar. He was also willing to look the other way when they left his church carrying what they found behind the sarcophagus.

Before the week was over, a sealed diplomatic package

containing the old leather suitcase arrived in Washington. Forensic experts determined that it had been manufactured in Oshkosh, Wisconsin, in the Thirties. The toilet articles, handkerchiefs, socks and underwear packed inside had been made in Italy. The clerical suit, hat, topcoat and shoes were of American origin. All the articles of clothing would have fit a younger Father Alex Samozvanyetz.

Professor Sloane called Herb Coogan in Cleveland.

"We're done here, Herb. We've checked everything we could check and the Attorney General doesn't see any reason to keep Father Samozvanyetz incommunicado any longer."

"You don't have any reservations?"

"Well, I admit all that 'Will of God' stuff was hard for me to swallow, but the AG feels his story is plausible. Whatever happened, happened. We don't know why and I supposes Divine Providence is as good an answer as any other. So as far as we're concerned, the Jesuit Provincial can release Father Samozvanyetz from the infirmary and let him rejoin the living."

"Well, okay, I'll make the call," said Coogan.

"You sound less than enthusiastic, Herb. You have some reservations about this guy?"

"Nothing specific. Just a gut feeling that something's not right. I'll make the call, but I'll be keeping an eye on the situation and see what happens."

"If anything," said Sloane. "Staying alert never hurts. While you're nosing around, Herb, if you happen to run across God's will, please be sure to send me a copy."

AT MASS IN THE main chapel that Sunday morning, Father Samozvanyetz was introduced to all the Jesuit priests, scholastics, brothers and novices at Milford. The Rector recounted how the Jesuit priest, while visiting Poland, had been caught up in the chaos of World War II and somehow ended up imprisoned in the Soviet Union. His brief account was short on specific detail.

What was important, said the Rector, was that he had survived the ordeal suffered by many other victims of Communist oppression and that God had brought him home from exile and imprisonment to Milford. It was now the job of his fellow Jesuits to help him recuperate, physically and emotionally.

Father Samozvanyetz stood silently, head bowed, before expressing his joy at being allowed to come home. He had gone through hard times but, thanks to God and the American government, that part of his life was over. From now on he hoped to lead a quiet life of poverty, chastity and obedience in the company of his fellow Jesuits. He had no wish for special treatment. It would take time, he knew, to adjust to community life after many years of living in spiritual isolation. It would be dangerous for him to dwell on the past and he would appreciate not being tempted to revisit it.

Finally, he expressed his love for Russia, for the Russian people, even for his Soviet captors. He prayed daily, he said, not only for the members of the Church of Silence but also for those who persecuted the faithful. He then made the

Sign the Cross and in Russian invoked the blessing of the Father and of the Son and of the Holy Ghost. To which his fellow Jesuits responded: "Amen."

Then, in English, he intoned: "Savior of the World!"

The novices, scholastics, priests and brothers responded: "Save Russia!"

Again and louder: "Savior of the World!"

"Save Russia!"

The organist struck a chord and the assembled Jesuits began singing: "Holy God, We Praise Thy Name!"

When that rousing recessional hymn ended, Father Alex Samozvanyetz, S.J., followed his fellow Jesuits out of the chapel, across the corridor and into the silent refectory where he found his chair at the breakfast table and his place in the Milford community for the very first time.

PROFESSOR SLOANE SPENT PART of that Sunday at Camp David in private conversation with President John F. Kennedy and his brother, Robert. The President and the Attorney General listened to Sloane's assessment of Father Samozvanyetz and had some questions, most of them about the Jesuit's account of his time spent in the Soviet prison camps and the Russian convicts he came to know there.

"Some had held important positions," Sloane reported. "The Jesuit did not name names, but I got the distinct impression that he learned a lot from them about the inner workings of the Kremlin. However, he was reluctant to discuss any of that."

The professor had expected that the Kennedy brothers would ask about the confessions the priest had heard in Siberia. But they did not get into that. At least, not while he was there.

CHAPTER · 14

ENOUGH TIME HAD PASSED at Milford, Father Beck decided one Friday evening, to write his letter to the Provincial as he had promised to do. He sat down at the desk in his office, took up his fountain pen, dated the sheet of stationery and wrote: 'Dear Father Novak,' and stopped. He sat back, pen in hand, for several minutes before putting his thoughts down on paper.

As promised, this will bring you up to date on Father Samozvanyetz since he moved into his room on Paters Row. He grows stronger each passing day. He's been more or less following the novices' routine: Meditation and Mass in the morning, Examen at Noon, etc. Some gardening or general yard work during the day. He's been brushing up on his Latin and Greek and I think he'll be ready to teach a class or two, soon. Or at least tutor some of the slower novices.

Two weekends ago, he started helping out at our parish church in Cincinnati. He goes there on Saturday to hear Confessions, stays at the rectory overnight

and takes one of the Sunday Masses. There is a car
and driver available, but he insists on taking the bus
downtown and back. "I wouldn't feel comfortable
being chauffeured around like a rich man," he told me.
So off he goes with nothing in his pocket but the exact
change for his bus fare. That leaves the rest of us to
ponder our own practice of poverty.

Not that he reproaches any of us. Far from it. He just
lives his life and pays no heed to any of our faults or
eccentricities of which we have an ample supply. We all
know he's rigorous in following the rules of the house
and the Society. Rigorous with himself, that is, but
absolutely tolerant of others. He is an easy man to live
with.

As to government concerns about any psychological
damage he may have sustained in the Soviet Union,
hypnotic suggestion or so-called 'brain-washing' or
some other mind-altering procedure, I see no evidence
of that. Quite the contrary. What I am seeing, I suspect,
is a humble man who's walking an elevated spiritual
path.

I am not his confessor. I can only judge his inner life
by the way he conducts himself in our community. In
that, I believe I observe true holiness. I served as his
acolyte one morning, early on. It was an experience
beyond words. Never have I seen a priest say Mass
with such reverence, such feeling for the drama of the
Eucharist.

Only time will tell, of course, but I'm becoming
more and more convinced that we may be dealing
with the real McCoy here. Alex Samozvanyetz is every
inch the perfect Jesuit and that's something I've never
encountered before. Needless to say, I'll be keeping my
eyes open.

Father Beck signed the letter and put the cap on his
fountain pen. He turned off his office desk lamp, picked up
his letter and walked through the door to his living quarters: a bedroom with a reading lamp, a comfortable arm
chair, a bookcase and a bathroom. He settled into his easy
chair and read the letter through. Did it need revision? If
it was effusive, so be it. He'd stated his true feelings accurately. But maybe he should sleep on it.

The next morning after Mass, Father Beck dropped his
letter down the mail slot at the end of the hall. Father Minister, who was in charge of the financial affairs of the community, weighed the letter, put a five-cent stamp on it and
sent it on its way.

FATHER SAMOZVANYETZ LEFT THE grounds of the novitiate that Saturday morning and walked three blocks to
the bus stop where he placed his valise on the sidewalk by
his feet and waited, lost in thought. There was not much
in the small black bag: his breviary, his good cassock, a
clean shirt, a clean set of underwear, a toothbrush and the

cigar box which contained his shaving kit. That was all he would need for his overnight stay at the rectory of the Jesuit church in Cincinnati.

He had spent the night sleeping with one eye open, as he did in the camps. Old fears had returned, but he had not tried to push them away. He had survived for more than his share of years because he had never ignored the vague warnings that something might be wrong. Or, at least, that something was not right.

The bus arrived on schedule and he was pleased that it was almost empty. He climbed aboard, dropped his coins into the fare box and took a seat halfway back. He did not want to be pulled into conversation with anybody this morning, so he took out his breviary. Reading his Office, he had found, kept people at a distance.

"*Quam magnifica sunt opera tua, Domine,*" read the Ninety-first Psalm. "How great are thy works, O Lord! Thy thoughts are exceedingly deep." The Latin flowed directly into English without passing through the Russian filter. That was good. He continued reading. His eyes tracked the Latin phrases, but his mind soon wandered from the text.

What was it he could not see? What was it he could not understand? His mind, as it did in times of stress and danger, was working now in Russian. He tried to review everything that he had done since coming to Milford. It had not been that difficult to settle into the routine. He had felt comfortable almost immediately and he could not recall any instance when he had not followed the rules and customs of the house perfectly.

Yet something was going wrong. Or, at least, something was changing.

John Beck had certainly changed. He could see that, now that he thought about it. How often had he looked up and found Beck watching him? Beck was not so accomplished a dissembler that he could conceal his scrutiny. No, Beck was watching him. He had not imagined those quickly averted eyes.

The more he thought about it, the more he could see that Beck was watching his every move, hanging on his every word like a prison guard who suspects something's up, but doesn't know exactly what. Had Beck observed some flaw, detected some fault? If so, he would have to identify it and correct it. His mind raced over the events of the past few weeks, but he could find nothing wrong. So intense was his self-examination, he almost stayed on the bus past his stop.

Enough, he commanded himself. Concentrate on the moment at hand. He walked along the street toward the rectory, looking up at the spires of the church. Today is what is important. Tomorrow's dawn may never come.

Saint Francis Xavier, the Jesuit church in Cincinnati, had been established before the Civil War to serve what became a large Catholic congregation. Over the years, as the city changed, descendants of the early parishioners moved to the suburbs, leaving behind the elderly, the immigrants and the poor to fill the pews and collection baskets on Sundays.

There were always visiting Catholic business people and tourists attending Sunday Masses and some people who worked downtown on weekends at hotels, restaurants and stores. But few of the suburbanite faithful ventured back into the city to go to Mass at Saint Xavier "for old times sake." Some Sunday mornings, the old church seemed half-empty and almost without purpose.

Saturday afternoons and evenings were different. Affluent, middle-class Catholics gravitated to the church from small towns and city suburbs in southern Ohio and even Kentucky. Saint Xavier, after all, was a Jesuit church where priests sat patiently in their confessional booths waiting to comfort and absolve the desperate. So many people came to confession each Saturday that the pastor and his two assistants had to be reinforced by Jesuit priests from the faculties of St. Francis Xavier High School and Xavier University and, as in the case of Father Alex Samozvanyetz, from Milford Novitiate.

When he arrived, he deposited his valise in one of the rectory's spare rooms, donned his cassock and went downstairs to share the noon meal with the pastor and his assistants. Later, breviary in hand, he went to the church to begin his ministry. In the sacristy, he opened a drawer, took out the purple stole that is the symbol of the priest's power to forgive sins in Christ's name. He kissed it before draping it around his neck.

He glanced at a white card thumbtacked to the wall. Someone with a fine hand had lettered a quotation from the Cure D'Ars who had been criticized for spending too much time with individual penitents: "I am responsible only for those confessions which I hear."

Well said, he thought. He would no more rush a penitent than he would hurry through the Mass. In all his activities, he kept to a measured pace. It was better that way.

He left the sacristy with eyes downcast and walked across the front of the church, past the side altar of the Blessed Virgin, past the life-sized figure of a pale, bloody Christ hanging on a dark wooden crucifix. At the center aisle, he turned and genuflected before the main altar where the Blessed Sacrament reposed in its golden tabernacle. At the far side of the church, he turned and walked up the aisle to his confessional booth halfway to the back of the church. The booth had three doors. The nameplate on the middle one read: "Visitor."

Before entering, he looked slowly about, surveying the whole church. The people waiting to have their confessions heard knelt apart from each other, solitary individuals scattered about in the twilight. Few of them, he knew, needed to refer to the sins listed in the back of their prayer books in order to examine their consciences. Few had to scrutinize their lives to uncover some minor imperfection. People so untroubled would have stayed in their suburban parishes.

The sinners who came to confession at Saint Xavier knew full well what they had to tell a priest. Most had agonized for days or weeks or even years until they found the courage to do so. But they had been afraid to seek forgiveness near their homes where priests or neighbors might recognize them. So these strangers, driven by the pain of their separation from God, had skulked downtown and slipped into the dark anonymity of the Jesuit church. They now knelt staring at the main altar beyond the Communion rail, trying hard to pray, working up the nerve to walk to the confessional.

Father Samozvanyetz stood for a moment, letting them become aware that he was there. Then he stepped inside, closed the "Visitor" door behind him, sat down on the padded bench and waited. Soon he would hear footsteps, then the door on the penitent's side of the booth open and close. He would slide back the soundproof panel by his shoulder to reveal the translucent, perforated partition. He would hear a person whose face he could not see clearly whisper: "Bless me, Father, for I have sinned."

He would wait a moment or two because most would have difficulty continuing. Softly, gently, he would ask: "How long has it been since your last confession?" Some could not remember.

He would take his time, asking his probing questions in a comforting murmur and waiting patiently until they were able to declare their secret shame. He would offer them assurance of God's love and encourage them to try to sin no more. Some he would have to prompt as they tried to recall the Act of Contrition they had memorized as children. Finally, he would bless them all and whisper the Latin words of absolution. And then he would say in English: "Your sins are forgiven. Go in peace and sin no more."

The penances he exacted were not severe. Some leaving his confessional knelt in a pew to say no more than an Our Father and three Hail Marys. Other penances took a bit longer. Now and then a penitent left the confessional and walked across the church to kneel at the altar of the Blessed Virgin and recite all five decades of the Rosary. Fifty Hail Marys in all. Someone sitting in the rear of the Jesuit church could easily identify the penitents who had received special attention from Father Samozvanyetz.

FOR THREE SATURDAYS NOW, Major Oksana Volkova had been sitting in the church, watching. No one had noticed her. Who, after all, would pay any attention to an old woman fingering her beads in one of the back pews? It was all so safe and so simple.

Already she had observed more than a dozen men and women whose sins were too grave to be taken lightly. She had watched them as they tucked away their rosary beads, left the church and went back into the world, confident that their shame was known only to God and a featureless Jesuit stranger who had no idea who they were. It would not be difficult to follow any of them and discover their names, their addresses, their occupations, the exact nature of their sins and with whom they had been committed.

Yes, she thought, a blackmailing operation was entirely possible. But that was not the game she had come to play. What pleased her was that everything seemed to be working as she had planned. How fortunate she was to have discovered Alex Samozvanyetz, so many years before, in a cell in Lubianka. Not only to have found him, but to have realized his potential.

She had always been frugal. It was not her nature to throw away anything that might prove useful at some later date. A woman who saved used paper clips in a shallow glass bowl on her office desk would never discard a captured American priest. She had spent two decades planning and training, but here she was in America with all the pieces in place, waiting for the game to begin.

CHAPTER 15

IT RAINED SUDDENLY THAT Saturday night. Thunder-clouds rumbled above Milford Novitiate and sent the priests scurrying from their recreation parlor to close all the windows on Paters Row.

"What about Father Sam's windows?" said one of the priests.

"I'll take care of them," said Father Beck. He hurried to his own quarters and pulled down the double-hung windows in his office and bedroom. Then, as thunder resounded through the building, he hustled along the second floor corridor.

The door to his friend's room was unlocked as was the custom of the house. He stepped inside and switched on the overhead light. He saw immediately that the windows were closed against the driving rain. Alex had shut them before he left that morning. There was no need to do anything.

But Father Beck hesitated, his hand on the light switch. His eyes darted about the room. He could see his reflection in one of the dark, rain-swept windows. Slowly, he closed the door behind him.

The room seemed to be uninhabited. Except for the crucifix above the bed, the walls were bare. The hard bed was covered with a thin gray blanket stretched taut. Beyond the foot of the bed, near one of the room's two windows, stood a plain wooden armchair where Alex probably did his reading. There was no floor lamp next to the chair. There was not one stick of furniture that couldn't have been found in any novitiate dormitory room. Not one personal item had been added to the spartan furnishings.

A tall wardrobe made of dark wood stood against the wall between the two windows. A "coffin," the novices called it. On the wall by the door to Father Beck's right, there was a porcelain washbasin. The overhead light glinted off its metal fixtures.

Stepping farther into the room, Father Beck could see the mirror in a wooden frame that hung above the basin. Its reflecting surface had been turned to face the wall.

A low chest of drawers stood against the far wall, its top covered by a white cloth upon which were laid out a folded white bath towel, a face towel, a wash cloth and a bar of white soap in a metal dish. There was an empty space in the neat arrangement. Of course, thought Father Beck: Alex had taken his shaving kit with him into town.

He walked to the desk that stood between the chest of drawers and the window wall. It was the same type of school desk the novices sat at in their dormitories, a plain wooden desk with no drawers. Perched on top of the desk was a bookshelf, its back pressed flat against the wall. A straight-backed wooden chair was tucked in tight.

On the desk top there was a goose-necked lamp, the kind the novices used, two sharpened pencils, a wooden pen with a metal nib, a bottle of ink and a loose-leaf notebook.

The bookcase held three books: a Bible, *The Imitation of Christ* by Thomas A'Kempis and the second volume of Archbishop Goodier's *The Public Life of Our Lord Jesus Christ* which, according to the envelope attached to the inside of the back cover, had been withdrawn from the library earlier that week. Father Beck fingered the notebook for a moment, and then pulled his hand away.

Never had he seen a priest's room so bare and so austere. Except for the pencils and the pen, the books and the notebook, the towels and the bar of soap, the mirror with its face averted, the crucifix on the wall above the bed and the few pieces of necessary furniture, the room was empty. There was no clock on the wall, no rug upon the floor. There was not even a padded *prie-dieu* to kneel upon, only one of the rough wooden blocks the novices knelt on during their periods of prayer and meditation. Father Beck saw nothing in the room that was not community property.

He opened the door to the wardrobe. Inside, suspended from the wooden rod that ran the width of the coffin, he saw three empty clothes hangers, the old patched cassock that Alex wore around the house, a faded denim jacket and the work pants that went with it. On the floor of the wardrobe were a pair of work boots, a pair of worn felt slippers and, neatly folded, an empty laundry bag. The wardrobe held nothing that had not once been worn by some other Jesuits. Probably dead ones, thought Father Beck, as he closed the coffin door.

He slowly walked across the room to the chest of drawers. In the top drawer were four frayed but freshly laundered white shirts, four sets of underwear, two pairs of black stockings, two pairs of heavy woolen socks, and one Roman collar.

In the far right corner of the drawer were two spools of thread, one black and one white, and a thimble. A sewing needle was stuck in the black spool. The bottom drawer was empty, except for an old dark gray cardigan sweater.

Father Beck took one last look around the room. The man had not one item that could be called his own.

LATER THAT NIGHT, SITTING in his upholstered easy chair, Father Beck surveyed his own room: the clock, the lamps, the carpet, his bed with its comfortable mattress, the books he was keeping in his shelves, the gold fountain pen on his nightstand. He loved the fountain pen the women at the Provincial's office had given him when he left for Milford. It was his own fountain pen.

"Oh, come on, John!" he said to himself. "You're teetering on the brink of scrupulosity."

If Alex Samozvanyetz was a saint or well on the road to becoming one, he had no business comparing himself to him. He knew that. Alex was who he was. And he was just plain old John Beck. That's how God wanted things.

Still, he felt guilty. He had given way to curiosity. He had used the storm as an excuse to enter another's room without permission. It wasn't much of a sin. A fault, maybe, and not a terrible one at that. He had, after all, stopped short of opening Father Alex's notebook. He would mention his transgression to his confessor, of course. And he resolved never to do anything like that again.

Snooping was never a good thing to do. Especially in a cloister. But when he said his bedtime prayers that night, he couldn't help wincing at the words "forgive us our trespasses."

IT WAS LATE SUNDAY afternoon when Father Samozvanyetz returned from Cincinnati. He went directly to his room, closed his door and placed his valise on his bed. Then, as he always did after even the shortest absence, he stood motionless and let his eyes sweep across the floor, one row of tiles at a time.

He saw a short length of straw near the wardrobe, another in front of the chest of drawers. Two short lengths of straw. He picked them up and walked to the desk. The Goodier book had been opened; the others had not been disturbed.

He frowned at the two pieces of straw in his fingers and then placed them on the white cloth that covered the top of the chest of drawers. He finished unpacking and changed his clothes. He shook out his clerical suit and hung it in the wardrobe, along with the good cassock he wore when he said Mass.

Then, after shutting the wardrobe door, he put the two pieces of straw back in the bottom drawer of his chest where they belonged. The next time his room was searched, they would drop to the floor again.

That evening at recreation he acted as if nothing had happened. The only priest in the parlor who had difficulty meeting his eyes was John Beck. He pretended not to notice. Convincingly, he thought.

MAJOR VOLKOVA ARRIVED AT the Jesuit church early that following Saturday. Once again, she watched the priest leave the sacristy and make his way across the church to his confessional booth. But this time he carried his stole in his left hand, not draped around his neck. He had something to tell her.

She waited until there were only a very few people left in the church. Only then did she leave her pew and enter the priest's confessional. She knelt and waited for the panel to slide aside.

"I saw your signal," she whispered in Russian.

"There are things you must know," he said in a low voice. "Tuesday I received an invitation to a meeting in Washington the first week in July. Thursday a man from the White House telephoned and pressed me for an answer. He said the President wanted to meet me."

"You accepted, I hope."

"Yes, I knew you would want me to accept. The White House man said he would take care of travel arrangements. I had to tell the Rector because I needed his permission to make the trip. He has arranged for me to stay at Georgetown University."

"Will you be meeting the President face-to-face?"

"Only for a moment, I think."

"A moment is all that is required. I will send you a message tomorrow. I have information you will need about the President."

"I will watch for it. But I must tell you that John Beck searched my room last weekend."

"You are certain?"

"My markers were dislodged."

"Could he have found anything?"

"No. I keep nothing in my room."

"You are sure it was Beck? Not one of the others?"

"Yes, Beck. He has become extremely suspicious."

"Most unfortunate. Has he communicated his suspicions to anyone else?"

"I don't think so. He suspects something, but he is not certain of anything. Why else would he search my room, if not to find evidence to justify his suspicions? But he found nothing, so he will say nothing."

"We cannot assume that he will remain silent forever. Does he know you are meeting the President?"

"I am sure he will learn about it this week."

"Then he may tell his FBI friend about his suspicions, even if he has no evidence. One word from him can ruin everything. So Beck has to be eliminated. And quickly, too."

"Impossible!"

"I can make it look like an accident."

"No, it could not work. Too much commotion in a quiet place like Milford."

"But he must be silenced."

"Then leave him to me. I am certain I can handle this."

"You can eliminate him yourself?"

"I think I can silence him permanently. Give me two days."

"Two days, but no more. If you think your plan is not going to work, signal me immediately and I will take over. Do you understand? Beck must be silenced. If not by you, then by me."

"I understand."

"Very well," she said. "I must leave now."

"Yes, of course. Go in peace. But don't forget to say your penance."

"Don't be impudent."

"I am serious. You have been in here a long time. Say five decades of the rosary and be sure to look contrite. You never know who may be watching."

She cursed him in Russian and left.

CHAPTER 16

THE SUNDAY MORNING SUN, rising in a clear sky, dried out the air around Milford Novitiate and now it was just downright hot. Hotter than Hades, thought Father Beck. When his Mass in the main chapel ended, he knelt on the altar steps and prepared to lead the community in one of his favorite prayers.

"Saint Michael the Archangel!" he intoned. And the young men in the pews, the novices on the right side, the juniors on the left, responded forcefully:

"Defend us in battle. Be our protection against the malice and snares of the devil. Command him, Dear Lord, we humbly beseech You, and do Thou, O Prince of the Heavenly Host, by the power of God, thrust into hell Satan and all the other evil spirits who roam through the world seeking the ruin of souls. Amen."

LATER THAT MORNING IN the refectory, Father Beck toyed with his breakfast. The heat had taken away his appetite. He ate slowly and watched his silent novices attacking their corn bread and stew with gusto.

He liked that word *gusto*, a good Roman word, as strong as any words the Anglo-Saxons had made their own. In the same way, he liked the prayer to Saint Michael the Archangel. The prayer had gusto. You could zip right through it without thinking too much about its content.

Not that he doubted the existence of Michael and Lucifer and all the other angels and devils. He'd just never encountered any pure spirits in his lifetime, but that didn't prove that they weren't out there, somewhere, probably.

Their existence was an article of faith, of course. But Father Beck's spiritual life had always been more down-to-earth, becoming more mundane as he matured. As a small boy, he had been devoted to his own Guardian Angel whose small-framed image looked down upon him from his bedside wall. His name, he knew with childhood certainty, was Bill.

Was Bill still hanging around? Father Beck liked to think that maybe he was.

But even before his three years of theological studies, John Beck had come to regard pure spirits intellectually. He accepted the existence of angels much as he believed in the existence of gravity or torque or centrifugal force. As for the fallen angels? Well, Satan had never threatened him directly, not that he was aware of, probably because he'd never achieved a level of spirituality that might attract the Tempter's attention.

He recalled the shudder he felt when first seeing Salvador Dali's painting: "The Temptation of Saint Anthony."

The naked saint thrusting his crucifix against the horses of temptation might have been able to challenge the forces of evil tormenting him, but John Beck? A face-to-face encounter with even one of Lucifer's lesser lackeys would probably scare him to death.

What was it his old Master of Novices had said? "If you ever meet the Devil, he'll be wearing a black cassock." He had never been able to decode that remark. Maybe it didn't mean anything, he decided. But it had sure sounded profound.

He looked at the clock on the refectory wall. It was time for the bell to end the breakfast period. Father Beck arranged his knife and fork on his plate and sat back. The novices, he saw, had long since emptied the serving bowls and platters on their tables and were now waiting to stand and recite Grace after Meals in Latin.

For a moment, he considered joining the novices on their *Ambulatio*, but decided it was just too darn hot for a hike in the country. He would catch up on his paperwork and spend some time in the chapel instead.

AND SO IT WAS that Father Beck was in his office later that morning when Father Samozvanyetz telephoned from downtown Cincinnati.

"I'm glad you're there, John," he said. "I need to have a talk with you. Could you give me some time this afternoon?"

"Of course, Alex. Is something wrong? You sound troubled."

"You're right, I am troubled, John, and it would help me if you could hear my confession this afternoon. Would you be willing to do that for me?"

"Of course I would," said Father Beck.

"I don't know when I'll get there. I've been asked to say the eleven o'clock Mass, so I'll have my noon meal here before catching the bus back to Milford."

"Then I'll see you when you get here, Alex. I'll be waiting for you in my office."

FATHER BECK WENT TO the third-floor chapel which, he knew, would be empty until the novices returned from their *Ambulatio*. He knelt in prayer for a while and then sat down to think about the phone call.

What on earth would trouble a saint, he wondered? He had read about saints, of course, but he'd discounted a lot of the depictions of their inner lives as being overly pious. If Alex was troubled, it must be about something subtle, some minor fault or imperfection. Well, he would find out soon enough.

Father Beck doubted that he had much, if anything, to offer Alex Samozvanyetz in the way of spiritual guidance. But he had to admit that he was eager to be given even a glimpse of his friend's inner life. It might satisfy his curiosity or even confirm his suspicions about Alex's sanctity.

He closed his eyes and listened to his own breathing. Sometime later, he became aware of voices outside the building. The novices were returning from their hike. He knelt for one last prayer, asking God to help him help his friend. He felt a surge of confidence and happiness as he gazed at the tabernacle.

"I'll probably only have to dust off his wings a little," he murmured. "I think I can handle that. With Your help, of course, Lord."

FATHER SAMOZVANYETZ SETTLED INTO his seat on the bus to Milford and kept an eye on the other passengers now boarding. He recognized the young man wearing a sweatshirt and a Cincinnati Reds baseball cap who took a seat several rows behind him. The man would only ride for two stops, he knew, so he opened his Breviary and waited.

As the bus approached the second stop, the young man stooped beside his seat and stood up with an envelope in his outstretched hand.

"I think you dropped this, Father," he said just loud enough to be heard by anyone sitting nearby. Father Samozvanyetz accepted the envelope with thanks and slipped it into the inside breast pocket of his suit coat. He would wait to read his message in the privacy of his room, but he knew that it was his marching orders and what Oksana Volkova called her "secret weapon."

* * *

FATHER BECK SAT AT his desk reading his Office, silently reciting the prayers for the canonical hours of Sext, those hours from noon to three o'clock when the day's conflict between good and evil is supposed to be at its climax and the powers of Hell are supposed to have the greatest influence over mankind.

"They have all but put an end to me on the earth," the Psalmist was chanting, "but I have not forsaken your precepts." Father Beck was thinking, not about himself, but about his Savior who hung on the Cross through the dreadful hours of Sext while Satan brought all his forces to bear against Him.

Father Beck felt a presence. He looked up from his breviary.

His friend Alex was standing in the doorway, a dark figure wearing the good cassock he wore while celebrating Mass. His expression was grave.

"You are sure you are willing to accept this burden, John?"

"Of course I'm willing," said Father Beck. "I'll finish this later." Setting aside his breviary he removed his stole from the middle drawer of his desk. "Your burden can't be all that heavy, Alex."

"Don't take it lightly, John."

Father Beck kissed his stole and draped it around his neck.

"Just shut the door and sit down beside the desk, Alex. There's no need to kneel."

He lowered his eyes and waited.

He heard the click of the door latch and the faint rustle of his friend's cassock as he walked across the room and stood with his hands on the back of Father Beck's chair.

"I told you on the telephone that I am troubled. Deeply troubled. You said you would help me unburden myself. Is that correct?"

"Of course, Alex."

"You place yourself under the Seal of Confession with no reservations whatsoever?"

"Of course. Why do you ask?"

"Because there must be no mistake. What I tell you must be held secret forever. Nothing must be used by you in any way whatsoever. I desperately need that assurance, John, and you must not give it lightly."

"You have my assurance," said Father Beck with a smile. "I am certainly not going to break the Seal. Never."

"Even if you find you cannot give me absolution?"

"I don't see how that could happen," said Father Beck.

"But if it does, will you break the Seal?"

"Never, Alex. You have no need to worry so. I will never break the Seal of Confession."

"Very well. Then I shall begin."

Father Beck watched his friend sit down and arrange the folds of his cassock. Only then did he meet Father Beck's eyes.

"I have not told you the complete truth, John. But now that you are bound by the Seal of Confession, I shall."

Father Samozvanyetz took a deep breath and exhaled.

"I have no choice," he said. "Sometime last weekend you entered my room and searched it. Is that not correct?"

"Yes, that's correct." Father Beck lowered his eyes. "I am truly sorry about that, Alex."

"Yes, I'm sure you are. Or soon will be."

His friend sounded sad, disappointed.

"Look at me, John. Tell me what you see."

Father Beck clutched the arms of his chair. The room turned cold.

"What is happening?" he said. "What are you doing? I can't believe what I'm seeing!"

"You can believe it, John. Just keep watching."

"Something's happening to your face! What are you doing?"

"I am relaxing."

"Your face is falling away!"

"Something like that. An actor is leaving the stage and wiping off his make-up. Isn't that what you are seeing?"

"I don't understand."

"You are beginning to see what is real. Not what you have only imagined."

"Your voice is changing!"

"It is my real voice you are hearing. And your eyes are open wide now. Are you seeing what you have been looking for?"

"What is happening to you?"

"I am allowing myself to be myself."

Father Beck pushed back hard, shoving his chair away from the stranger before him.

"Dear God in Heaven! Who are you? You are not Alex!"

"Of course I'm not! You didn't know that?"

"What have you done with Alex?"

"God damn it, Beck! You didn't know? Then why the hell were you searching my room?"

Father Beck had retreated as far as he could.

"I was just looking around. It was raining. I went in to close your windows. I looked around. I'm sorry."

"What were you looking for?"

"Nothing. I was just curious."

"Just curious!"

The man slammed his fist into his hand, cursing in Russian.

"But you suspected me of something, Beck. You have been watching my every move. What did you suspect me of?"

"Not of being a fraud, an imposter! That never crossed my mind!"

"Then, what?"

"I believed you were who you said you were. I truly believed you were Alex! You took me in completely."

The man threw himself into the chair beside the desk.

"What a terrible, terrible, terrible mistake I have made!"

"For God's sake," Father Beck pleaded. "Tell me what you've done with Alex! Is he still alive in Russia?"

"No, he is dead. Some three years now."

Father Beck slumped in his chair.

"I see," he sighed.

"I am afraid you do not see, Beck. And you must see, for your sake as well as mine. You and I, we must go on, Beck. What is done is done and now there's no turning back.

"I have come to you to confess, remember? That is why I am here. I am confessing in order to keep you silent. So you must hear it all."

Father Beck stared at the stranger before him. He felt the Seal of Confession tightening around his chest.

CHAPTER · 17

"WHO ARE YOU?" FATHER Beck muttered.

"I am not Alex Samozvanyetz. My real name would mean even less to you than it does to me." The man shrugged. "I intend to keep the name I have now, so it will be better for you if that is the only name you know."

"It was all a lie! Everything you told us about Alex was a lie?"

"No, what I told you was true, except that it happened to Samozvanyetz, not to me. His capture, his imprisonment, his life in the camps: that was essentially true, just as I described it. His interior life, as well. What you heard is what you would have heard from his own lips. Of that, you can be sure. I heard it all from the man himself."

"You knew him, then?"

"It was my job to know him. Know him better than he knew himself. I spent years listening to him and studying his every word, every gesture, every mannerism, every memory. I lived with him in the prison camps. He thought I was a fellow prisoner. A fellow priest. A Russian priest of the Eastern Rite. He never doubted it."

"I don't understand," said Father Beck. "You are a priest?"

"No, I am not a priest, John. I was trained to play the part of the priest you knew."

Father Beck sat silently, shaking his head.

"How did Alex die?" he said at last. "Can you tell me that, at least? Did they execute him after all?"

"No, they did not. The cold, the work, the poor food. He died, exhausted finally, like so many others. There was not much left of him, except his spirit, I'm afraid."

"And he died without a priest?"

"I was with him. I heard his confession. I gave him the Last Rites, just as I was trained to do."

"Monstrous!" said Father Beck.

"Not at all. He believed I was priest. What's important is what he believed, wouldn't you say? He seemed content to leave this world and he did not die alone."

"Because you were with him? A false priest and a false friend?"

"It could have been worse. He could have died without anyone. Even a counterfeit priest is better than none at all. Believe me, Beck, I played my role very carefully, to the very end of his life. I wanted to give him some comfort in his last hours.

"I respected him, you see. He was a good man. Intelligent, kind, generous. But, in the end, he died. And I took over his name and identity."

He stood up.

"You look ill. Let me get you a glass of water."

"I'll get it myself," snapped Father Beck.

He tried, but there was more strength in his voice than in his body. He had to accept the man's help to get to his feet. He staggered to his bathroom and vomited in the washbasin. When he was finished, the man wiped his mouth with a wet washcloth, then moved him aside and rinsed out the bowl.

"You will feel better now," he said. "Wash your face in cold water. It will clear your head. You've had quite a shock, I know."

Father Beck did as he was told. He dried his face with a towel and glared at the reflection of the man's face in the mirror.

"I see that you are angry. That's good, John. We can deal with reality now."

He took Father Beck's arm and guided him back to his desk and settled him into his chair. The man took off his own cassock and threw it over the back of his own chair, rolled up his shirtsleeves and sat down.

"Listen carefully, John. You know the truth about how Samozvanyetz got to the Soviet Union. Now I will tell you what you do not know. After your friend was apprehended and imprisoned in Lubianka, he was held by the NKVD and undoubtedly would have been shot.

"But a young, ambitious Red Army lieutenant named Oksana Volkova intervened in his case. She was interrogating military prisoners who had been sent to Lubianka for political reasons when she stumbled upon Alex Samoz-vanyetz.

"Lieutenant Volkova believed he should be kept alive. She could not say exactly why, but she believed that an American Jesuit might prove useful someday in the future. She successfully argued that he was, in a technical way, a military prisoner. So she took charge of his case and was able to keep him isolated in a special section of Lubianka. She had no plan then, I believe. She was just following her instincts. Until, that is, she found me.

"Now, about myself," he said. "I was born in Saint Petersburg and raised in Leningrad, as people of my generation say. Before the war, I was an actor: not well known, but slowly building my reputation. When Germany invaded my country, I was conscripted into the Red Army.

"I had no military training, but I became a good enough soldier. There's nothing an actor can't learn to do in three weeks and I learned enough to survive many battles. Many of my comrades and officers were killed, so I rose through the ranks to a position of command.

"One night, the Germans overran my company. We were cut off for several days, but some of us managed to fight our way back to our own lines. Our battalion commander welcomed us enthusiastically, but some damned political officer charged us with desertion. He claimed that we had gone over to the Germans of our own free will.

"So, one day I was a hero of the Red Army and the next day I was a traitor being hauled off to prison in a boxcar.

Fortunately, my first interrogator was Oksana Volkova, who was by now a captain in the GRU. By chance, she had seen me on stage some years before and remembered my performance.

"But she said nothing about that during my first interrogation. She was cold and correct, and never let on that she recognized me. She sent me back to my cell and to the prison routine so that I would learn who had the power of life and death. She probed, investigated, questioned everything about me for almost a year. Only then, when she was convinced that I knew I was completely in her power, did she take me into her confidence.

"What would it take, she asked me, for a trained actor such as myself to become another person? Not on the stage, but in life? Not for two hours, but for a lifetime? Could such a thing be accomplished?

"The idea intrigued me. I replied that the actor would have to know a great deal about the other person, much more than he would have to know to portray a character on stage. Then there would be the matter of physical resemblance. Theatrical make-up only works at a distance.

"She took me to observe the man she had in mind. That is when I first saw Alex Samozvanyetz. At that time, I knew nothing about his true identity. I watched him from behind a one-way mirror during one of his interrogations. I studied him as best I could after that, watched more interrogations, watched him through the peephole of his cell door.

"What I saw immediately were his eyes. Just like mine, they were. He could have been a member of my own family. Our chins were similar, too. It was not that close a resemblance, I thought, but Oksana Volkova believed it was close enough to work with."

The man turned his head to show Father Beck his profile.

"I don't look all that much like him, do I?"

"No, only in a general way," said Father Beck. "I can't understand how I was taken in so completely."

"Don't rebuke yourself. You were an excellent audience. The very best. Attentive, generous with your emotions, eager to believe. A good audience sees what it wants to see."

He smiled as if he were complimenting a small child.

"Preparation was the key to it all. Oksana Volkova worked hard for years to make it possible for you and the other Jesuits here to suspend disbelief.

"First the letter from Russia and the photos. Then I appeared: an actor who had spent long, hard years of study and rehearsal preparing for this one performance.

"What I lacked in physical resemblance had to be made up for by specific detail in speech and movement."

He snapped open his right hand, looked down at the outstretched fingers, then quickly looked up.

"That's Samozvanyetz making a point, is it not?"

He dropped his hand to his knee and looked down at his shoe.

"Samozvanyetz modestly accepts a compliment. Just as you remember."

The man rubbed the left side of his chin.

"Perfect, yes?"

He looked up and grinned at Father Beck.

"Alex searching for a thought. One of a thousand movements, signs and gestures. And how many quirks of speech? Oksana Volkova collected them all and I made them my own. By the time she completed her interrogations, I learned everything of importance that there was to know about Alex Samozvanyetz and I absorbed his life like a sponge."

"Alex would never have cooperated of his own free will," said Father Beck. "Was he tortured?"

"No, never. It was not necessary. Oksana Volkova knew from the very first interrogation that he would die rather than betray anyone. That, she perceived, was his greatest fear. So that is what she used to get what she wanted.

"She led him to believe that she was trying to turn him, to make him her agent, to send him out as a Judas goat to lead innocents to slaughter. She knew, of course, that he would never go out among the Russian Catholics as her agent, her spy, her informer. But he didn't know that she knew. He was deathly afraid that she might succeed in turning him by trickery or torture.

"So, to prevent her, to divert her, to relieve the pressure, he talked and talked and talked. Like the woman Scheherazade telling a thousand and one tales, he told her in great detail all sorts of personal anecdotes and experiences. He was trying to keep her at bay by giving her hours of facts and stories he believed could hurt no one. And she was recording everything that she really wanted me to know.

"He poured out all his memories about his training as a Jesuit, about his dear old friend John Beck. It took a full five years, but Oksana Volkova drew out of him a complete autobiography rich in detail. Five years, John! And never, once, was he aware of what she was doing! Brilliant, wouldn't you say?"

Father Beck struggled weakly in his chair, but he couldn't escape the man's words that pounded away at him like hammers. He tried to breathe, but his chest ached. For a moment, he thought he was going to suffocate.

"Are you going to vomit again? Do you want a glass of water?"

Father Beck tried to wave him away.

"Here, drink a little of this."

Father Beck's hands trembled when he tried to take the glass. The man held it to his lips. He sipped a little water, shamed by his own helplessness.

"That's better," said the man. "You are in shock, I know. But you have to hear and understand all of this. It is important and necessary, believe me."

Father Beck could say nothing. He watched the man walk to the window. He grasped the arms of his chair and tried to rise, but he lacked the strength. He sank back into his chair and lethargy engulfed him. The man sat down again next to Father Beck's desk.

"I know this is distasteful and painful for you, but you

must bear with me. I must tell it all. While Oksana Volkova was milking Samozvanyetz's memory, she established me in a suite of rooms in a building outside the prison. Only a few people she trusted were allowed to enter. Technically, I was no longer a prisoner, but I was not free to move about either. I lived there and studied there. I suppose you could call it my seminary.

"My first task was to learn English well enough to read it. I started with copies of the primers used in the grammar school Samozvanyetz had attended. My reading got better with practice. But Oksana Volkova ordered me not to attempt to speak the language. That, she told me, would have to come later.

"There were several rooms in Volkova's seminary: my living quarters where I slept and took my meals, the library where I studied everything that Samozvanyetz had ever studied in the United States and in Rome, a small room where I looked at motion pictures, and a larger room fitted out as a church where I practiced Roman Catholic rituals and also those of the Eastern Rite.

"How Oksana Volkova got it all assembled, I don't know. But she accumulated everything needed for my research and preparation: books, films, vestments, candles, incense, everything. And how diligently I studied: Latin, Greek, Italian, American English, philosophy, theology, the history of the Roman Catholic Church and the Society of Jesus.

"My memory has always been good and I was a superior

student when I was young, but the schooling Oksana Volkova put me through almost broke my head.

"When I was not studying, I was reading the books Samozvanyetz said he had read. I read old American newspapers, studied old photographs of Samozvanyetz and his family and of the places he had lived. Oksana Volkova had found pictures of every place he said he had been and pictures of almost every person he said he had known.

"She made me watch hours and hours of motion pictures: priests saying Mass, leading processions, baptizing babies, giving sermons, walking through towns and cities, talking to people on the street. Not theatrical films. They were of no use, whatsoever. I studied hundreds of documentary films and amateur films. Any picture that showed any American priest doing anything at all. I would watch the priests closely and then I would imitate them. All the rituals are described in the Rubrics, as you know, but seeing them performed in real life was a great help to me. And, then, of course, there was the man himself to study.

"When I completed my seminary training to Oksana Volkova's satisfaction, I was sent to join Samozvanyetz in the labor camps. This was the most difficult part of my preparation, but she felt there was no other way. We lived side by side, Samozvanyetz and I, as fellow prisoners and fellow priests. So he believed, and why wouldn't he? I was every inch a priest and, in the camps, I received no special treatment.

"He was more than happy to help me learn to speak

English and over our time together I learned how to speak the language exactly the way he did. And the way he spoke Russian as well. He was an excellent teacher and he taught me more than he could ever imagine. I was able to absorb his speech patterns, his walk, his mannerisms, all of which were being changed by the hardships we were undergoing.

"Those were long, hard years. But that's when he revealed all the deeper parts of himself that he had never revealed before. As well as his thoughts and his attitudes which were changing, day by day, as he drew closer to the end."

The man looked at the crucifix above Father Beck's desk.

"He was a most impressive man, Samozvanyetz. His spirit never broke. Only his body."

"You just let him die?"

"There was nothing I could do to help him."

"And this woman Volkova? There was nothing she could do?"

"No, there was nothing she could do. The Red Army did not run the camps. The internal security people were in charge. She was lucky just to be able to get me into the camps and get me out. No, there was nothing she could do to make things easier for Samozvanyetz or even for me. That's the way it had to be. It was necessary."

"I don't understand," said Father Beck.

"Why should you? There were two intelligence services in the Soviet Union, the political NKVD and the military GRU. The Red Army struggled to make sure there were two so that there would never be just one. The NKVD and the GRU kept each other in check, more or less, and they despised each other. So Oksana Volkova's superiors in the Red Army knew her project had to remain secret to protect it from the politicians. The NKVD is called the KGB nowadays, but that secrecy is still necessary.

"After Samozvanyetz died, Oksana Volkova pulled me out of the camps and got me back to Moscow. It took a while to recuperate physically, but I don't think I will ever get over the degradation of the experience. But I have to accept the fact that Oksana Volkova was correct.

"Acting has its limits. It would not have been possible for me to assume the identity of Alex Samozvanyetz without having endured what he endured. His suffering is a part of me now.

"So, he died. Well, we all die, do we not? But I would have to say that he was more fortunate than most of us, for he died with all his illusions intact. You might say that Oksana Volkova kept Father Samozvanyetz's faith alive, if only for purposes of study. He lived longer than he would have lived had not Oksana Volkova intervened at Lubianka. And, thanks to her, Samozvanyetz was able to do some of what you Jesuits had trained him to do. It is true! He ministered to the other prisoners and that was important to him. He believed he did some good. His mind was at peace when he died, judging from what he told me in his last confession."

"Stop!" cried Father Beck. "Have you no decency?"

"Contain yourself, John. I have no intention of breaking the Seal of Confession, counterfeit though it may be. I know that you couldn't take that blow. I simply want to reassure you that your friend died a good Jesuit. One you can be proud of. I'll say no more about it."

"Good," said Father Beck. Anger was clearing his mind. "Why did you agree to do all this?"

"I had no choice. Believe me, I had no choice then and I have no choice now."

"Are we finished now?"

'Not yet. There is more that you have to know. While I was continuing my studies and training in Moscow, negotiations for the visit of the American agricultural group began, at which time Oksana Volkova planted me at a state farm so that I could be discovered. Her scheme worked perfectly, for here I am."

"But why? What are you trying to accomplish? There's nothing of value to you here."

"Nothing at Milford? Of course there is. Perfect cover. A quiet place to sit and wait."

"Wait for what?"

"For what, indeed? For information, John. That is what the GRU gathers all over the world, at all places and at all times. Information is a commodity, like oil or coal or gold. And Oksana Volkova believes that a priest might collect the most valuable information of all."

"Why are you telling me all this? You know I am not going absolve you. But, then, you don't want absolution, do you?"

"No, I don't want your absolution. I have what I want. Your silence.

"Listen to me, John. Oksana Volkova wanted you dead. I convinced her that your death was not necessary. All we needed was your silence and we have that now, do we not?"

Father Beck did not reply.

"I have given you enough information to destroy me, to send me to the firing squad or the electric chair. But I know that you will not use it because you cannot. You cannot reveal any of this information or use it in any way. Is that not correct? You cannot betray me, can you? Answer me!"

"No, I can't betray you."

"There is one last thing you must not reveal, John. I have been invited to go to Washington to meet the President."

"Oh, my God!"

"Do not worry. I will not harm him. My job is just to listen, remember?"

"I wish you had listened to that Oksana woman," said Father Beck. "I would be better off dead."

"That can always be arranged."

The man picked up his cassock from the back of his chair and put it on. He wrapped his cincture around his waist and pulled it tight.

"I respect you, John Beck, and I trust you. But prudence demands that I keep a close watch, lest you give way to human weakness."

He walked to the door and stopped.

"Look at me," he commanded. "Don't forget for a moment that your life is in danger, as well as your soul."

The man turned around to face the door, paused for a moment, then turned back again.

There stood Father Alex Samozvanyetz, S.J.

"Please, John," he said in that familiar voice, "do not do anything stupid while I'm gone."

With that, the man who played the part of Father Alex Samozvanyetz left Father Beck's office, closing the door behind him.

The latch clicked softly. Father Beck shuddered. He knew his prison cell door had been slammed shut. He could not move or think. He raised his eyes to the crucifix on the wall above him, but he could not pray. Like Alex Samozvanyetz in Lubianka, he had been condemned to a life of solitary confinement. Like the suffering Christ on the Cross, he was alone in the world, forsaken by his Father, cut off from all help.

THE SUN WAS SETTING. Out in the corridor, the electric bells rang. It was time for Litanies and Benediction in the main chapel.

Father Beck pushed his chair back from his desk and stood up. He would have to carry on and act as if nothing had happened. God and the Russian agent would be watching him.

He worked hard to finish his supper that Sunday evening. It was the usual simple meal: bread, soup, cold cuts, potato salad, Jell-O for dessert. He had no appetite. He was afraid of calling attention to himself in any way, so he forced himself to eat.

Thank God, it was a silent meal. One of the juniors was reading aloud from the pulpit set between the swinging kitchen doors at the far end of the refectory. Father Beck, eating mechanically, had no idea what book was being read. The words were meaningless to him.

When supper ended, he joined the other priests in the second floor parlor for recreation because he was expected to be there. He did not contribute to the general conversation, but pretended to listen attentively, nodding or smiling or laughing when it seemed appropriate.

He tried to ignore the man who pretended to be Alex Samozvanyetz, but he couldn't help himself. The man was mesmerizing. Even knowing the truth, it was difficult to see through the actor's performance. And now this Russian spy had John Beck performing, too. He began to feel light-headed, almost giddy.

He seemed to be looking down upon the room from a great distance watching himself and the imposter. Could he leave early? The recreation period was drawing to a close. He yawned and walked toward the door, but the Rector intercepted him.

"Has Samozvanyetz told you he's going to Washington next week?"

Father Beck didn't know what to say, so he raised his eyebrows and said nothing.

"He's going to meet the President," said the Rector. "Pretty exciting, isn't it?"

"Yes, very exciting," said Father Beck.

"Are you feeling all right, John?"

"I'm just a little tired. I'm going to turn in early."

Father Beck escaped to his room. The brief exchange had terrified him.

He sank down in the easy chair by his bed. Here, at least, in the solitude and privacy of his own quarters, he was in no danger of saying or doing the wrong thing. He was caught in a trap. There was nothing he could do without breaking the Seal of Confession.

But what about *breaking* the Seal? He tried without success to rid himself of the ugly question.

Why couldn't he be as cynical as the man who had trapped him? Informing the authorities would be a mortal sin, a pre-meditated sacrilege. But couldn't any sin be forgiven if one repents?

But would he repent? If he intentionally cut himself off from God's grace, would he ever be able to regain it? Or would he be dragged farther from salvation like a swimmer caught in a strong current?

Was he being too scrupulous? Would a single mortal sin be such a terrible blot on a lifetime record? Wouldn't a just and merciful God consider the extenuating circumstances?

He had been tricked and maybe it was God's will that he risk damnation to fight such evil? God only knew what this false priest planned for the President of the United States!

Father Beck rushed from his chair to scan his book-shelves, but he knew there was no book anywhere with an

Imprimatur and a *Nihil Obstat* that would set him free. He must remain silent. He had been rendered powerless to do anything except put on his pajamas, brush his teeth and go to bed.

SO WHERE WAS BRASH, glib John Beck now, he asked himself. That happy-go-lucky fool was sitting in his pajamas, head bowed in despair, crushed by his secret burden, condemned to silence or damnation. Silence or damnation. John Beck's only choices.

He tried to kneel, but crumpled to the floor beside his bed. His fingers clutched the bedspread.

"Alex!" he sobbed. "Help me, Alex!"

CHAPTER · 18

THE MAN WHO PLAYED Father Samozvanyetz spent a restless night in the Jesuit residence at Georgetown University. He woke up that morning with a dry mouth and queasy stomach, something he had often experienced before opening-night performances.

He breathed deeply and quietly vocalized as he showered and shaved and dressed. As always, his stage fright evaporated this morning as he stepped through the door and onto the Washington stage.

The President of Georgetown and the Provincial of the Maryland Province delivered him to the White House well in advance of his ten o'clock appointment with President Kennedy. He felt comfortable enough to feign polite interest in the furniture and paintings the young presidential aide pointed out as he guided the Jesuit visitors through the White House and into a parlor near the President's office.

There were a few other visitors gathered there, all civilians, chatting nervously. He had no difficult identifying the two Secret Service bodyguards. They were calm and had nothing at all to say.

Two men with cameras arrived and were immediately allowed into the Oval Office. Good, he thought. The photographers might provide him with a moment alone with the President. Perhaps by taking a photo of the two of them shaking hands? A moment was all he needed. He resisted the urge to put his hand in his pocket. Bodyguards are trained to notice such mistakes.

His first impression of the Oval Office was that it was smaller than it appeared in the pictures Oksana Volkova had given him to study. But the dark blues, the golden draperies, the polished wood, the sunlit carpet with its presidential seal all heightened the desired effect of understated power.

The furnishings and decorations directed a visitor's eye to the presidential desk. Off to the side of a conversational grouping of comfortable sofas and armchairs stood the President's celebrated rocking chair with its cushioned seat and back.

"Quite impressive, isn't it, Father?" whispered the Maryland Provincial.

"Indeed it is," he replied in a hushed tone that indicated the correct amount of awe. "I never dreamed I would ever be here."

He felt the dramatic tension intensify. The guests had been given just enough time to allow anticipation to reach its zenith. Then the presidential aides stopped making small talk and turned to the door through which the President would enter.

All eyes followed. A hush fell over the room. Eight seconds later, the door swung open.

President John F. Kennedy stepped into the Oval Office and advanced toward his audience with his Irish teeth and hair and eyes, the not-quite-straight posture, the confident stride with just the slightest hint of pain. The man who played Father Samozvanyetz joined in the visitors' applause for a perfect entrance any actor would admire. He sensed that the Oval Office had become brighter. Was it charisma or lighting?

Shamelessly, the President of the United States waved aside the small ovation he had elicited.

"Good morning, Reverend Fathers, Ladies, Gentlemen!" he said with a smile.

The man who played Father Samozvanyetz responded with all the others in the room, "Good morning, Mister President!"

President Kennedy walked directly to him, clasped his right hand and held it with both hands.

"Welcome to the White House, Father Samozvanyetz! We're all extremely happy that we were able to bring you home."

"Thank you, Mister President," he replied. "I am deeply appreciative."

"I'm told you've been able to settle into a comfortable routine?"

"Yes, Mister President. A quiet and ordinary life, thanks to you. May I introduce my companions?"

"Oh, I know them very well, Father. You travel with some notorious characters."

The President freed his hand ending their moment alone.

"We seem to be overrun with Jesuits today," the President said to the other visitors. "Let's hope our Southern Baptist friends don't get wind of this. It will confirm their darkest suspicions."

This was, of course, a joke. He could see that his Jesuit escorts were delighted by the President's playfulness. But the man who played Father Samozvanyetz only smiled politely and did not join in the laughter. A man so long out of touch would not appreciate such a reference.

He noticed that President Kennedy had noted his lack of reaction.

While the President moved on to greet the other visitors, shaking hands and chatting, the man who played Father Samozvanyetz stood listening to the medley of easy banter, friendly teasing and respectful rejoinders. He smiled pleasantly, presenting an air of mild bewilderment, but not disapproval.

He was surprised when the President returned to him and guided him to the chair next to his rocker and waited until he sat down before taking a seat himself.

The other visitors were directed to the perimeter of the Oval Office where they watched out of earshot. The photographers moved forward and took several pictures of the serious young President focusing all his attention on the Jesuit priest sitting before him.

The photographers stepped away and President Kennedy spoke quietly. "Please stay seated while the others leave, Father."

The man who played Father Samozvanyetz watched John F. Kennedy pose for photos of him shaking hands, one by one, with all the other visitors. When that ritual concluded, the President thanked his guests for having visited and allowed his aides to usher them out of the Oval Office.

The two Jesuits seemed flustered and a bit unhappy about being ushered out to the lobby while the priest they had brought to the show remained, as it were, backstage with the star.

So far so good, he thought.

The two Secret Service agents were standing apart at a discreet distance. Both, he saw, would have a clear shot if it proved necessary.

The President, having left his charm on the stage, returned to his rocking chair.

"I've been reading the transcript of your debriefing with considerable interest, Father Samozvanyetz. I want to ask you directly about certain details. Rather, certain omissions."

Good. He was getting down to serious business.

"You did meet former Soviet officials in the labor camps?"

"That is correct, Mister President. A great many."

"Knowledgeable people? Former high-level officials?"

"Yes, Mister President. Several of the very highest level."

"And they told you things," said the President.

It was a statement, not a question. So the man who played Father Samozvanyetz drew back slightly.

"I have a problem discussing this, sir."

"I understand, Father. This is not the time or place to explore such a delicate matter. But I want to get a sense of how restricted any further discussion might be."

The man who played Father Samozvanyetz looked down at his folded hands to conceal the excitement he felt. Wait, he told himself. Say nothing. Just listen. The President of the United States was leaning forward now.

"Please believe me, Father Samozvanyetz. I would never ask you to do anything that would violate your conscience. I am, however, deeply concerned about the probability of a serious miscalculation by either the Soviet Union or the United States. I believe it is inevitable. We don't understand each other very well, if at all. I believe it is inevitable that one of us is going to make a serious mistake. Do you agree?"

"I am afraid that I do, sir."

"Might it then be possible, within limits we both understand, that you might give me your insights, impressions or even just opinions about how the present leaders of the Soviet Union might be thinking?"

The man who played Father Samozvanyetz took his time answering.

"I would have to be extremely careful, Mister President. Some things I can never reveal."

"I understand. I know I am asking you to walk a very thin line, Father. But could you, at least, think about it?"

The man who played Father Samozvanyetz glanced at the Oval Office door as if searching for a way out. How far the President was prepared to go? He decided to find out and looked the President in the eye.

"Could you guarantee that such consultations would be private? Just the two of us? Face to face?"

"Yes, I could guarantee that."

The man who played Father Samozvanyetz pursed his lips as if he were pondering the matter. He let the pause play out, then spoke slowly and deliberately.

"I will give this serious consideration, Mister President. Your concerns are completely justified. Perhaps I can find some way to help you."

"That's all I need to hear today, Father. We'll talk again."

The President grasped the arms of his rocking chair. The man who played Father Samozvanyetz saw the flash of real pain in President Kennedy's eyes as he pushed himself out of his rocking chair and rose to his feet. The President shook his hand and the private conversation was over.

One of the Secret Service agents held the door open. The man who played Father Samozvanyetz walked out of the Oval office and joined the two Jesuit superiors who were waiting for him.

"Is there anything you care to tell us, Father?" asked the President of Georgetown.

He shook his head and the two Jesuits nodded.

"Then we had best move on," said the Maryland Provincial. Another polite young presidential aide swept them through the corridors of power and out to the White House driveway.

THAT NIGHT, BACK IN his room in Milford, he took Oksana Volkova's secret weapon out of his suit coat pocket. It was a sheet of note paper, folded again and again so that it could fit into the palm of his right hand, small enough to be transferred during a handshake without anyone noticing but disturbing enough to cause the President to ask himself: "How did he learn about this? And what else does he know?"

The man who played Father Samozvanyetz unfolded the paper and put a match to it. He let it burn over his sink, turned on the faucet and watched the ashes disappear down the drain.

The way the meeting played out, there had been no need to use the list Oksana Volkova had delivered to him. Nor would there be in the future. He had stored the names of all six women in his memory where he could recall them, just in case.

That Saturday morning, the man who played Father Samozvanyetz, acting as if nothing unusual had happened that week, took the bus downtown to hear more confessions at the Jesuit church.

CHAPTER · 19

FATHER BECK LABORED AT his desk that morning, forcing himself to personalize the form letters to the young men who would make up the new class of Jesuit novices. What had once been a pleasant task was now a joyless chore. He saved the most agonizing letter until last, the one to Herb Coogan's son.

"My Dear Charles," he wrote in the space above the typewritten text.

> Our Very Reverend Father Provincial has notified me that he has passed favorably on your application for admission to the Novitiate. Allow me to congratulate you, and to assure you of a warm welcome to Milford. The enclosed papers should be of help.
>
> I would advise you to get some expert help in marking down your cassock measurements, which should be returned to me as soon as possible. A good tailor can help our lay brothers avoid errors which can sometimes be costly and annoying. It would be wise, also, to visit both a dentist and an oculist if you have

not done so recently. Any attention you may happen
to need can be had now more conveniently than in the
early weeks of the Novitiate.

We will be expecting you on August 21. In the
meantime, I pray that our Dear Lord will have you in
His good keeping, and that He will bring you safely to
our doors after a pleasant vacation.

In the space above his typewritten title "Master of Novices," he wrote: "Very sincerely yours in Christ, John Beck,
S.J." He folded Charley's letter and its mimeographed at-
tachments in thirds, the way the nuns had taught him in
grammar school, and slipped them into the last envelope.

If only he could have written to all of the young men:
"Stay away! Don't leave your homes! I am in no condition
to receive you, let alone start you off on your spiritual journey!" Warning them off, of course, was impossible. There
was no way to stop them.

NOTHING HAD PREPARED JOHN Beck for the anguish
of isolation he would now have to endure. He was locked
in a spiritual prison and had no way to find release. His
life had suddenly gone terribly wrong. All he could do was
look back on his life and ask God: "Why me?" Hadn't he
done everything right?

Nourished by unselfish parental love, his boyhood had
been bright and happy. He enjoyed classroom routine and

excelled in his schoolwork. He was a quick learner, facile but not brilliant. His teachers and his classmates liked him. He passed through an athletic adolescence unruffled by anxieties that troubled other teenagers.

He was popular; he had good friends, but never a best friend or a best girl. He knew, somehow, that he was just passing through his classmates' lives, that he was on his way out of their small Midwestern town and was never coming back.

It was not until his junior year at the University of St. Louis that he began to feel the calling to become a Jesuit. But by the time he won his Bachelor's degree, the United States had entered the First World War and twenty-one year-old John Beck enlisted in the Army. He served less than two years and was never sent overseas. He spent another two years in St. Louis trying to become interested in the business world and found that he could not.

When John Beck arrived at the Jesuit novitiate, he was a mature, self-aware young man of good character. Just the kind of fellow they seemed to be looking for. From his first day as a novice, he felt as comfortable as a dolphin in the sea. The vows of poverty, chastity and obedience, which he took two years later, freed him completely from the pull of worldly gravity. He had found his natural habitat and he rode the spiritual waves and currents without effort. Jesuits who had lived with John Beck in community called him a "natural." Like a DiMaggio, they said, he was born to play the game.

The vow of poverty posed no problems for John Beck. He had never worried much about material things. He drew his clothing from the Society's general stock, never asked for anything special and took what he was given. Yet his cassocks and suits always fit perfectly.

The vow of obedience never troubled him. If anything, it was liberating. The rules of the Society, he found, were reasonable and wise. No superior had ever asked him to do anything that was wrong or even foolish. There were times he felt the need to voice an objection or disagreement. But once his superiors made their decisions? Well, that was it. Obeying his superiors was obeying God.

He knew the vow of chastity troubled others, but he seldom thought much about it. He never felt that he had missed out on something important or given up anything of value. Hearing confessions taught him how easily men and women could be swept away by passion. But that was something he had never experienced himself. When he was younger, he was aware that women had found him attractive. He was always puzzled by their attention, but never intrigued.

He responded to women with friendly indifference as zebras might acknowledge gazelles who shared their same grasslands, similar but inherently different, beautiful as all God's creatures are beautiful, but of no particular interest. He respectfully moved aside to give them space to graze. He knew they were there, but he had no urge to seek intimacy. Much less, prey upon them.

Truth to tell, he had always felt that way about most people, men as well as women: respectful, appreciative but somewhat detached. He was, he supposed, a solitary creature. But he had never been lonely in the Society. There were always good people around, the kind of people, thank goodness, who had learned to respect his privacy. They knew how to keep their distance and not intrude. But now, suddenly, everything had changed.

Now he had to distance himself while maintaining the appearance of collegiality. He had to follow the regular community routine with his fellow priests. He had to shepherd his novices, prepare them for their meditations, hear their confessions, instruct them on the ideals of the Society of Jesus and explain the implications of the vows to be taken at the end of their novitiate.

He had to do all that without giving the Jesuits with whom he lived the slightest inkling of the invisible chains that were crushing his spirit. The Seal of Confession kept him from calling out to them for the relief he so desperately desired.

Father Beck pressed his fingers into his temples. His eyes were sore and his head ached. His vision was a little off. Eye strain, probably. Was he coming down with something? A summer cold? Maybe he should see Brother Hegstad in the infirmary and get something to ward it off.

He felt the tightening of the muscles in his back and shoulders again. It was hard to catch his breath. The room was spinning. He stumbled into his bathroom and reached the toilet just in time to throw up his supper.

LATE THAT SATURDAY EVENING, Oksana Volkova slipped into the confessional booth at the Jesuit church in Cincinnati to listen to her agent's report.

"He wants to consult me about what I learned in the camps."

"Excellent! I knew he would not be able to resist. He will never let go of you now."

"But I am not certain that he will ask me to reveal what I heard in confessions."

"He will if he thinks the stakes are high enough. He is a practical man, not a religious fanatic."

"He seemed to be sincere about his faith."

"Of course he did. He is a politician. Also, he is an adulterer. Did you use my information?"

"No. I decided not to use the names you gave me."

"That was wise," she said. "It would have been excessive. He does not have to believe that you are a clairvoyant or a mystic. He just needs to believe that you possess valuable information which he cannot have. You will never be very far from his mind."

"What do I do now?"

"Nothing. Wait for him to make contact with you. When that will be, there is no way of knowing. A month? A year? No matter. He is worth waiting for. But should I worry about John Beck?"

"No, not at all. When I confronted him about his behavior, he apologized for examining my room. He had been looking for evidence that I was some sort of saint. I denied it and asked him to keep his suspicions to himself. I am sure that he will."

FATHER BECK HAD MANAGED to get into his bed and fall to sleep that night. But he was wide awake at three o'clock in the morning.

"Why am I still alive?" he whispered to himself.

He was alone in his room in the dead of night, staring up into the darkness, a useless bystander witnessing calamity and unable to intervene or even sound a warning. He was becoming powerless to do any good for anybody here on earth and fearful that he was lost in a cold, unconcerned universe with no discernable purpose.

"What have I done with my life?" he asked himself over and over in the night. "Why am I still alive? Why can't I just die?"

Red Army Spies
and
the Blackrobes

continues in Book Two:

DAYS OF DANGER

About the Author

PATRICK TRESE, an original staff member of the *Huntley-Brinkley Report*, was born in Detroit during the Depression and raised in Cleveland during the second World War. Hiroshima and Nagasaki were destroyed when he was a junior in high school and the Cold War began.

Trese was not drafted until 1953 but by that time he had finished high school, spent a year as a Jesuit novice, left and finished college and wrote sports for the local NBC radio station. The fighting in Korea ended about the time Trese finished his 18-week basic infantry training. The Army assigned him to write for the Armed Forces Press Service in New York where the young soldiers, sailors and airmen watched the Army-McCarthy hearings on TV.

During his 30 years at NBC News, he shared several Emmys and a Peabody for "Tornado! Xenia, Ohio" which showed how a local newspaper helped this small town recover from sudden disaster. (*The Gazette* won a Pulitzer.)

His book about making documentary films in Antarctica in 1957-58, *Penguins Have Square Eyes*, was published in 1962.

Caril, the story of Caril Ann Fugate, who became involved with mass-murderer Charles Starkweather and was convicted of first-degree murder at age 15, was published in 1972. It was based on his NBC News prime-time investigative documentary "Growing Up In Prison."

After retirement, he wrote the 10-part PBS series "America Goes to War," narrated by Eric Sevareid, and 12 episodes of "The 20th Century" series narrated by Mike Wallace.

Bitter Medicine, which he co-authored with Richard E. Kessler, MD, dramatized how the doctor used malpractice cases as teaching tools for his medical students.

54075309R00137

Made in the USA
Middletown, DE
12 July 2019